A Player's Practice

I had no interest in learning to feign stabbing with a dagger on the stage, but Will's enthusiasm was infectious. "Now, with my back to the audience, I thrust the dagger toward you, like this, and it slips under your arm, and then you squeeze the bag of blood that you've concealed beneath your costume, and—"

Will lunged, and I moved my arm aside so that the make-believe dagger would pass under it. But I must have moved the wrong way, or Will miscalculated; in either case we collided, and I lost my balance and toppled over backward. Will stumbled and fell forward. We landed in a tangled heap on the grass, his face just inches above mine. We stared at each other. And then he kissed me.

I was the first to come to my senses. I pushed him away and scrambled to my feet, breathless. *What am I doing here with this boy?*

"Pray pardon, Anne!" Will cried, blushing. "I crave your forgiveness, I never intended—," he stammered.

"Never mind what you intended," I said crossly and clamped my arms across my chest. "I've had enough of your instruction in stage fighting."

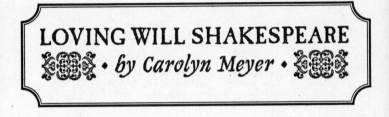

LOVING WILL SHAKESPEARE
· by Carolyn Meyer ·

Harcourt, Inc.
Orlando Austin New York San Diego London

www.HarcourtBooks.com

First Harcourt paperback edition 2008

The Library of Congress has cataloged the hardcover edition as follows:
Meyer, Carolyn, 1935–
Loving Will Shakespeare/Carolyn Meyer.
p. cm.
Summary: In Stratford-upon-Avon in the sixteenth century, Anne Hathaway suffers
her stepmother's cruelty and yearns for love and escape, finally finding it in the arms
of a boy she has grown up with, William Shakespeare.
1. Hathaway, Anne, 1556?–1623—Juvenile fiction.   2. Shakespeare, William 1564–1616—
Juvenile fiction.   [1. Hathaway, Anne, 1556?–1623—Fiction.   2. Shakespeare, William,
1564–1616—Fiction.   3. Stepmothers—Fiction.   4. Country life—England—Fiction.
5. Great Britain—History—Elizabeth, 1558–1603—Fiction.]   I. Title.
PZ7.M5685Lov   2006
[Fic]—dc22   2005033188
ISBN 978-0-15-205451-9
ISBN 978-0-15-206221-7 pb

Text set in Adobe Garamond
Designed by Lauren Rille

DOM   10 9 8 7 6 5 4 3 2

4500237914

Printed in the United States of America

Loving Will Shakespeare is a work of fiction based on historical figures and events.
Some details have been altered to enhance the story.

• This one is for Tony •

STRATFORD-UPON-AVON
•*Warwickshire, England 1611*•

My dear Anne,
I am coming home. I shall soon leave London and
return to Stratford-upon-Avon to live and work
for the rest of my days.

ILLIAM SHAKESPEARE, the most famous poet and playwright in all England, has written these words to me. Will Shakespeare—able to move audiences to tears as easily as to laughter with tales of love and lust, jealousy and honor, loyalty and betrayal—coming home at last! Can it be so? I have read his letter a dozen times over, and after all these years, I scarcely know whether to laugh or cry. Now, as I await his return, I have decided to set down the story of our life, Will's and mine, from its beginnings.

CHAPTER ONE
•The Black Death•

E MEASURED our days by the ringing of bells—bells calling us to Sunday worship, sounding the close of the Thursday market, warning us off the streets at the nightly curfew. Joyfully pealing bells heralded weddings and christenings. Muffled, mournful bells announced deaths.

In the terrible year of 1564—the year the plague swept across England—the death knell tolled more than two hundred times in Stratford-upon-Avon, our town of some fifteen hundred souls a hundred miles from London. Here in the heart of Warwickshire the Black Death carried away one life of every seven, leaving six behind to grieve.

On the twenty-sixth of April in that year, before the plague and the fear that traveled with it had reached us, our family attended the christening of the firstborn son of John and Mary Shakespeare at Holy Trinity Church. Standing by the stone font, Vicar Bretchgirdle poured holy water over the infant's head and named him William.

The Shakespeares were well known in Stratford. John was a glove-maker and wool-trader, and Mary a daughter of the prosperous Arden family. Thanks to his wife's inheritance of property in the nearby village of Wilmcote, John was a man of means. Mary Shakespeare and my mother had been dear friends from childhood, and when the service had ended and the bells rang out, our family was among the well-wishers invited to call at the Shakespeare home next to John's shop in Henley Street.

Mary, still pale from the rigors of childbirth three days earlier, rested on a wooden settle made comfortable with pillows. Next to her the babe lay in a handsome cradle. His mother watched over him tenderly as John received their friends. The table in the parlor was spread with a white linen cloth on which fine pewter servers were heaped with meat pies, aniseed cakes, and marchpane. Guests drank to the health of the infant. He had slept through most of the goings-on and now suddenly awoke, wailing lustily. I stood by the cradle and rocked it gently, as I'd often rocked my infant sister. But the babe howled even louder, until his mother picked him up.

That was my first introduction to Will Shakespeare. I was seven years of age.

There were five in my family: my father, Richard Hathaway, a yeoman farmer; my mother, Agnes, for whom I was named; my ten-year-old brother, Bartholomew, whom we called Tolly; my sister, Catherine, called Catty, barely a twelvemonth; and I. We lived at Hewlands Farm in the hamlet of Shottery, two miles from Stratford by the field path. Our thatched and half-timbered cottage sat amid lush gardens, blossoming orchards, fields of barley, and pasturage for flocks of sheep and goats, a team of oxen as well as a few cows and horses, and a garth clamoring with chickens, ducks, and geese.

Within weeks of William Shakespeare's christening, our lives changed in ways I could not then have imagined. The plague arrived in our town, the seeds carried, it was believed, by an apprentice lately come down from London. In July the vicar entered in his burial book the Latin words *Hic incepit pestis:* "Here begins the plague."

Just days past my eighth birthday on August first, Mary Shakespeare came to Hewlands Farm to talk to my mother. She said that she was taking the infant William to stay at her family home in Wilmcote until the danger was past and urged my mother to move me and my sister, Catty, to safety. "For their sake, and for the sake of your unborn babe!" Mary begged. My mother's belly was already big with her sixth child—two had died in infancy before Catty was born. This one was due in November.

I remember the loveliness of that day. Warm sunshine and a gentle breeze teased the delicate blue flowers of the flax field as the two women walked together in my mother's herb garden, Mary pleading, my mother making an effort to be cheerful.

"But where would we go?" my mother asked. "There's none of my family left in Billesley. Besides, we're as safe here at Hewlands as you will be in Wilmcote. Surely we must trust God to protect us, wherever we are." She didn't mention her two dead infants or Mary's two, turned to dust in the churchyard.

The friends embraced and kissed each other, and Mary Shakespeare took up her swaddled infant William, whom I'd been holding as they talked. She carried him away, while my mother waved to her bravely from our garden gate. I clutched her hand and wept, fearful that my mother was wrong, that we were not safe.

The death knell continued to toll. Fires were built in the streets to drive away the pestilence, and we carried flowers and sweet herbs in our pockets to protect ourselves from bad odors that carried the disease. Yet, despite the danger, the law required everyone to be present at church each Sunday. Obediently we took our accustomed places and listened as Vicar Bretchgirdle exhorted us from the pulpit to rid ourselves of the sin that he believed to be at the root of the plague.

"The Black Death is God's vengeance upon His disobedient people!" the vicar thundered. My parents glanced fearfully round the church, remarking the number of empty seats, wondering who among us might be carrying the seeds that could infect us and who might next be struck down. Later, at our Sabbath meal, my father and mother spoke of those absent, among them our nearest neighbors, Fulke and Martha Sandells and their daughter, Emma, who was my closest friend. Emma and I were nearly the same age. Fulke and Martha had stood as godparents at my christening, my parents at hers. Often we walked together to Holy Trinity and home again after the worship.

"I'll go over today and see about them," my mother said. "Mayhap they're ill," she worried. "Martha has never been strong."

"Nay," my father said firmly. "I'll go." He fixed me with a stern eye when he saw that I meant to go with him, eager to see Emma. "Agnes," he said, "stay here with your mother."

He returned with the welcome news that all was well with our neighbors. "Fulke says he'll keep his family at home, away from the pestilence, regardless of the law. He says he'll pay the fine, if it comes to that."

"Mayhap he's right," my mother suggested.

But the next Sunday we attended church as usual.

❦

There was no harvest festival that year, on account of the plague. We offered grateful prayers that we had survived thus far and went about our lives as best we could. When the nights grew cold, my mother and I sat by the fire, distaff of wool in one hand, drop spindle in the other, while she taught me how to draw out the fibers and twist them into yarn. Catty slumbered on her pallet nearby.

One evening in October, when the first heavy frost was expected and my father and Tolly had gone out to see to the lambs, my mother complained of a headache and laid aside her spinning. Even the light of a single rush candle seemed too bright for her to bear. By the time my father and brother had come in from the sheep-fold, she was trembling with fever and chills.

For the next few days I scarcely left my mother's bed-side. Too frightened to weep, I did what I could for her, bathing her face with cool cloths dipped in lavender water, bringing her barley water to swallow when she was able. Swellings appeared on her body, under her arms and on her neck, and she cried out from the pain. My mother writhed and raved as the swellings grew larger— as big as my fist—then turned black and finally burst, and the reeking pus poured out of them. I prayed passionately for her recovery, but as her suffering increased and nothing brought her relief, I began to pray even more earnestly for her merciful death. That prayer was soon answered, and the solemn bell tolled once more.

The vicar, exhausted by the ordeals he witnessed day after day, spoke the words over my mother's body, wrapped in a linen winding-sheet. Tolly stood by my father's side, rigid as iron. I held Catty in my arms, so weakened by my sorrow that I feared I might drop her. By God's grace the rest of us had been spared, but our mother had taken with her the babe in her womb.

It was a desolate time for us at Hewlands. Our neighbors were so fearful of the plague that they refused to come near us. Sometimes Martha Sandells sent a few loaves of bread or a round of cheese wrapped in cloth to be left where I would find them, but Emma was forbidden to visit me, and I was not allowed there. My father and brother buried their sorrow in work, while I felt alone in my misery, scarcely able to care for Catty, or even for myself.

❧

The gravediggers could not keep pace with the need. There was no space left in the churchyard to bury the stinking corpses. Once during the awful weeks after my mother's death, as I hurried past the church on an errand with my father, I witnessed men with kerchiefs covering their mouths, digging open the old graves. To make room for the newly dead, they hauled out the whitened bones, the grinning skulls, the ragged tatters of the shrouds in which the bodies had long been buried. Others dragged the gruesome remains to the charnel house behind the church, throwing the bones into tangled heaps. Though my father tried to shield me from the dreadful sight, for many nights my dreams were haunted by what I had seen and by what I imagined. I awoke screaming in terror, my heart pounding, convinced that I, too, would be flung into the charnel house among the bones of the dead while I was still alive and breathing.

When the deep cold of winter lessened the danger, Mary Shakespeare and Will returned from Wilmcote. Soon after Twelfth Night she came again to Hewlands Farm, bringing her bright-eyed son, now out of infant swaddling and dressed in a little russet gown. When she saw how sad and thin I had become, my hair uncombed and the household in disarray, she burst into anguished tears. "Oh, how sorry I am!" Mary cried. Will crawled on the filthy rushes covering the flagstone floor until his mother took him up again on her knee.

"Agnes," she said, clasping my hand in hers, "I once had a daughter just two years younger than you who lived but a few precious weeks, and then a second daughter whom God allowed to remain with us less than a twelvemonth. I dream of again having a little girl in my home. Mayhap it would be easier for you and your father if Catty came to stay with us. I would be happy to care for her until you're ready to have her with you again. 'Tis the least I can do to honor your poor mother."

Take Catty away? I could not bear to lose my sister, too! I looked anxiously to my father, who had entered the hall to accept Mary Shakespeare's condolences and now sat staring at his calloused hands clenched in hard fists upon his knees. He shook his head slowly.

"I'm grateful to you, Mary," said my father, his voice still clotted with the grief of our loss. "But we'll manage somehow."

Mary Shakespeare nodded. "Aye, Dick," she replied. "With God's help you will." Then she turned to me, pushed a straggle of hair out of my eyes, and said tenderly, "If ever I can be a comfort to you, dear Agnes, I hope you will come to me."

I nodded, doubting I ever would. I liked Mistress Shakespeare but my yearning for my own mother was something Mary could not satisfy.

We struggled on for a few more months with only one indolent maidservant to help. Through the blusters of winter my father did what he could, but with the arrival of spring, he spent nearly all of his time birthing the new lambs and then planting the field crops. Finally, I suppose, my father recognized that we couldn't manage after all, and he devised a solution.

He decided to take a new wife.

❧

I knew nothing of my father's decision to marry until I sat beside him in church on the first Sunday after Easter. Before the sermon Vicar Bretchgirdle read out an announcement in his deep, deliberate voice: "I publish the banns of matrimony between Richard Hathaway of Shottery, widower, and Joan Biddle of Drayton, widow, for the first time. If any of you know cause, or just impediment, why these two persons should not—"

My mouth fell open. Stunned as I was, I didn't hear the rest of the vicar's words but turned to my father and tugged at his sleeve. With bent head he studied his thumbs and paid me no notice.

Through the remainder of the service I stole furtive glances at the faces of the women in the congregation. Drayton was a hamlet not far from Shottery, and my eye fell first on one woman without a husband by her side, then another. *Is it that one, in the gray bonnet? Or the one with three little ones climbing on her lap?*

As soon as the service ended and we left the church, I began to pester my father with questions. "You'll meet her soon enough," he replied impatiently. "Her husband and only child have also been lost to the Black Death." That was all he had to say on the subject, and I left off asking.

I wanted desperately to talk to someone about what was happening, but there was only Tolly, and Tolly was no help. "He planted a flax field," my brother said, "so it seems he plans to bring a new wife to our home to spin it. He doesn't speak to me about such matters."

On a Tuesday after the third reading of the banns my father brushed his breeches and doublet, washed his face, put on a clean shirt, and left home without explanation. I watched him leave, an uneasy feeling in the pit of my stomach. I guessed that he was on his way to wed and wondered in what ways our lives would now change. Later that afternoon he returned, bringing his bride straight from the church.

"This is your stepmother," he said as she stooped to enter the hall through the low doorway. "See that you mind her."

Joan was a tall, sallow-faced woman with one eye that wandered off course while the other peered straight ahead. Her manner was abrupt, her voice loud and grating. I was angry. Where had he met her? Why had he married her? When I later put these questions to my brother, Tolly shrugged and said, "'Man needs a wife,' that's what Father told me." I looked up to my older brother, but he generally kept his thoughts to himself and had few words to offer on any subject. My own thoughts were that we could have managed well enough without this woman or any other, but particularly without this one.

On the morning after her wedding Joan announced that her first task was to see her new home put in good order by Whitsunday. She tied an apron over her plain woolen petticoat and bodice, tucked her thin, brown hair under a white linen cap, and set about the task with grim determination.

She assigned me to sweep out the filthy rushes that covered the floors, scrub the flagstones, and strew over them fresh rushes mixed with pennyroyal to ward off fleas and sweet fennel to keep evil at bay. She enlisted Tolly to whitewash the walls with lime. Panes in the latticed windows were cleared of layers of grime and cob-webs. Iron kitchen pots were scoured with sand. The dresser was polished with beeswax.

For days we worked steadily to accomplish what had been left undone for months, pausing only for the sim-plest of meals—a chunk of coarse raveled bread, a dish of pottage, a pot of ale. Joan had me rip open our flock mattresses and stuff them with handfuls of fresh wool. She set my father to replacing the ropes in their bed-stead. On the walls of our hall she hung the painted cloths brought from her former home, so that we ate and slept surrounded by scenes of brave Daniel facing the lions and mighty Samson bringing down the walls of the temple. My father built a wall cupboard in which to display her three or four pieces of good pewter and a single brass candlestick, which I polished with crushed eggshells and goose fat. There was no question that whatever Joan set her mind to would be accomplished. She offered neither thanks nor encouragement but lib-eral criticism.

"Did your mother teach you nothing?" my step-mother bawled at me one afternoon. "Or are you merely a lazy sloven who refuses to learn?"

"My mother taught me to spin and to take honey from the bees and many other things as well—mayhap more than you could know!" I dared retort.

"But not to speak respectfully, I see. Mayhap going without supper will correct that," she replied.

"I believe I hate her," I told my brother glumly as I lay exhausted—and hungry—on my pallet.

"Won't do you naught of good," Tolly replied, slipping me a bit of bread and cheese he'd saved from his own meal. "But neither would loving her. 'Tis all the same to her."

By Whitsuntide, as she'd ordered, we finished our tasks, and Joan moved on to her next duty: to provide my father with a number of children. By Midsummer Night our stepmother was expecting their first child. Toward the end of March of the following year, Tolly rode to Stratford-upon-Avon to fetch the midwife; three days later an infant girl was carried to Holy Trinity for christening. They named her Joan. My father took to calling his new daughter Joan Little, and eventually so did we all.

CHAPTER TWO
·Stepmother·

EEDS OF prickly discontent must have sprouted in my heart during the hollow months that followed my mother's death. By the time of my father's marriage to Joan, the discontent had taken root. My belief that our lives would change proved true, and I resented the changes. As the months passed, the discontent grew into a troublesome plant, like stinging nettle that inflicts pain with even the slightest touch. My stepmother found fault with everything I did and punished me.

"I do try, Tolly," I told my brother when I had again been banished from the table, this time for allowing the watery gruel to burn, though not so much it could not be eaten. "But nothing ever satisfies her."

"Nor will it," Tolly said. "You're too much like our mother. Father looks at you and can't help but remember her blue eyes and fair hair. Stepmother knows that and can't forgive you for it."

Though it pleased me that I resembled my mother, I saw that, if Tolly was right, the likeness would continue to cause me trouble.

Joan was a shrewd woman who brought a tidy sum of money to the marriage and was bound to make the most of it. Her dead husband, Biddle, had been a maltster, in the business of converting barley to the malt used to make ale. After she wed my father, Joan sold the malthouse to her brother, Martin Ingram. With that money she had my father build a small alehouse behind the cottage, and she bought a little pied pony and a two-wheeled cart. My mother had brewed enough ale each week to supply our household. Joan increased the amount by severalfold and sold what we didn't need. Soon she had established a thriving trade.

I was expected to help with the ale-making, hard work I didn't enjoy. More to my liking was the chore of delivering ale to Joan's customers in Stratford as well as in our own village and nearby Drayton. Twice each week I loaded the cart with earthenware jugs packed in straw and set out before dawn on the rough and rutted road to Stratford-upon-Avon.

My first stop was at the home of John Shakespeare, at that time the town's official ale-taster whose duty was to assure the quality of the drink. Several ale carts waited in the Gild Pits, a muddy thoroughfare that ran behind the Shakespeare house. John came out from his breakfast, greeting us with a hearty "Good morrow to you!" Choosing one jug at random from each of us, he poured a sample into the pewter tasting cup on a chain round his neck and took a swallow or two.

Mary Shakespeare often came out to embrace me. "Does all go well with you, dear Agnes?"

"Aye, thanks be to God."

Will, peeking from behind his mother's petticoats, smiled up at me. Given half a chance, he chattered away merrily until his mother hushed him. "He talks nineteen to the dozen, this one does," she said, beaming and stroking his curls. Will's infant brother, Gilbert, gurgled contentedly in the crook of her arm.

My rounds included some of the grandest homes in Stratford—well-to-do mercers and woolen drapers, and even one or two gentlemen—as well as the new vicar of Holy Trinity, William Smart. I dealt with the servants, who exchanged empty jugs for full ones and paid me the penny owed. The maids were all great tattlers who kept me abreast of the latest gossip. My deliveries began to take longer and longer.

Twice each month I drove to the malthouse in Drayton. I sometimes stayed to watch Joan's brother and his two sons at their labors, turning the sprouting barley with long rakes and shoveling it into the malt kiln to dry. Then one of the sons loaded the sacks of malt onto the cart, and I dawdled home again, always to find my stepmother complaining loudly of the delay.

❦

In April of 1569 Mary Shakespeare gave birth to the daughter she'd longed for, and our family attended the christening of their infant, Joan. Afterward at Henley Street, Will, who would observe his fifth birthday in a week's time, made himself the center of attention, reciting a rather long poem that he had memorized for the occasion. Later, we walked back to Shottery along the field path through the newly planted barley—my father and stepmother, Tolly, Catty, and Joan Little, who at the age of three was turning out to be as sour-faced and ill-tempered as her mother.

"Couldn't bring herself to serve my ale, now could she?" complained my father's wife.

"Doubtless the Shakespeares buy from several different brewers," my father reminded her.

"Mine's better than their watery stuff," my stepmother snorted, and continued to grumble the whole way home.

❧

Not many months later our own family increased by the birth of a boy, named Thomas. Now there were seven of us occupying our three-room cottage, plus our shepherd, Thomas Whittington, a maidservant or two, and, depending upon the season, several laborers; sometimes as many as a dozen people slept there. The large hall was open to the rafters; smoke from the stone hearth found its way out through a blackened hole in the thatched roof. We took our meals at a trestle table that was dismantled and moved out of the way once we'd eaten. We also slept in this hall—the parents in the tester bed, the infant in a cradle, the other children on pallets pushed aside during the day. Servants and hirelings slept in a small chamber over the kitchen among sacks of grain and barrels of dried apples.

My father decided to enlarge the cottage. He had a chimney stack built above the hearth and hired Joan's brother-in-law, Samuel Fletcher, a carpenter from Stratford-upon-Avon, to lay a wooden floor over the oak beams of the hall. This added a bedchamber on the upper floor, where the tester bed and cradle were moved.

We now had four rooms and were less crowded. Even so, there was no escaping Joan's baleful eye.

I was always happier out of doors, where my growing restlessness was soothed by the warmth of the sun on my face and the smell of damp earth beneath my feet. I cultivated a vegetable garden, helped with the haying, pulled the flax, and took special delight in tending the bees that had been my mother's pride. The summer I passed my fourteenth year I rented a stall at the weekly market in Stratford-upon-Avon.

Every Thursday, country people from miles distant crowded the market cross in High Street: peasants in smocks, blue-coated apprentices, yeomen in flat caps, housewives with willow baskets on their arms. Sellers hawked their wares: butter, cheese, and eggs; capons and ducks alive and squawking; bloody slabs of meat; heaps of vegetables and fruits in season. I offered not only honey in the comb for sale but also lavender cut fresh from the fields or dried. My beeswax was much in demand as polish because of its pleasant scent. I sometimes made a few beeswax candles for the wealthy families who could afford them. (Ordinary folk burned rush candles—rushes dipped in scalding fat. They were ill-smelling and short-lasting but cheap.) The time at the market passed quickly.

At home, though, I clashed often with my stepmother, who continued to find numerous faults: I failed to pluck the pinfeathers from the hen in the stewpot, overlooked eggs in the nests until they were addled, carelessly broke two earthenware jugs—among countless other blunders. One day I crossed the brook to Fulke Sandells's farm to borrow salt for brining, fell into a conversation with Emma, and forgot the bread dough I was to knead once it had risen. When I finally remembered it, the dough had sat too long. Joan greeted me, brandishing a long-handled wooden spoon, and chased me round and round, occasionally managing to land a smack on my buttocks, blows I scarcely felt through my thick woolen petticoats.

"You're certain to come to a sorry end, my lass! What decent fellow will ever want you for a wife, eh? Answer me that!" she bellowed, puffing after me, the blood boiling red in her usually sallow face.

"If the likes of you can find a husband, then anyone can!" I cried, and immediately regretted it.

Joan's jaw dropped. In a fury she lashed out at me, striking me hard across my face with the wooden spoon. We stared at each other, Joan's jaw gaping, my fingers touching my flaming cheek. Then, howling with rage and pain, I turned and fled to the barn and flung myself at Tolly.

"How now, sister!" my brother exclaimed, grasping me by the shoulders. Tolly at sixteen favored our father with his broad chest, stout limbs, deep-set eyes, and deliberate speech.

I poured out my woes, and Tolly listened sympathetically. "One of these days you'll be gone from here," he said. "And these unhappy times will be forgotten."

"But how am I to live in the meantime?" I wailed.

"'Tis for you to decide," he said. "You can be her enemy and make yourself miserable by it, or you can endure it. If 'twere me, I'd choose endurance."

But I could not, for the life of me, think how I was to do that.

❦

Lambing season falls near Lady Day, the twenty-fifth of March, a time of unsettled weather between the last bitter blasts of winter and the first mild breaths of spring. My father and Tolly and Shepherd Thomas were spending night and day in the barn with the pregnant ewes. My stepmother, who usually helped with the lambing, had been called to Stratford to tend her sister, Alys Fletcher, the carpenter's wife. Alys's newborn babe had come too soon and was clinging to life by a slender thread. Joan had been gone for two days, taking Joan Little and my brother Tom with her. Catty and I reveled in her absence, singing as we went about chores that now seemed lighter. But on the third night I was shaken awake by my father.

"Get up, Agnes," he whispered hoarsely. "I need you. The lambs are coming too fast, and some of the ewes are troubled. I'm here alone."

"Where's Tolly? And Shepherd Thomas?"

"With Fulke Sandells. He came by an hour ago, begging help in finding several ewes missing from his sheepfold. You're needed *now,*" he added gruffly. "Make haste."

Climbing past the sleeping Catty, I pulled on two heavy petticoats, thrust my feet into wood-soled pattens, threw a shawl over my shoulders, and followed my father to the barn. I could hear the bleating of the laboring animals before we reached the lambing shed. By the light of Father's lantern I counted at least a dozen ewes with their newborns, the tiny creatures already nuzzling at their mothers' teats.

"Some first-time mothers have a harder time," Father explained, "and a few of them have their babes coming the wrong way, hind parts first. If the lamb is stuck, we might lose both lamb and ewe. 'Tis your small hands I need now, to turn the lamb inside the ewe."

I stared for a moment at my father. I had never done this. "But—," I began.

"Go on," urged my father, holding the lantern high.

Crouching in the cold shed, I reached inside the ewe. The tips of my fingers moved along the spine of the unborn animal until I felt what I believed to be its head, and I attempted to turn the creature inside the mother's womb. The ewe complained loudly.

"I cannot," I told my father.

"Take hold of the feet." I felt for the tiny hoofs and grasped them. "Now pull."

The hoofs slipped out of my fingers. I tried again, and failed again. "I cannot," I repeated after my third attempt, tears of frustration coursing down my face.

"Aye, you can, Agnes," Father insisted.

This time, despite my clumsiness, the lamb slid out into the world. I sat back on my heels and wiped my face on my sleeve as the ewe began to lick her newborn. Within minutes the wet lambkin tottered to its feet.

"Well done," said my father, his hand solid on my shoulder. "There are others. Come."

Some of the new mothers seemed not to have the least idea of what to do with their new offspring, pushing them away in annoyance when the small heads and eager mouths nudged against their swollen udders. So I whistled to them softly, a tune that seemed to soothe them both, until finally the ewe understood what she must do.

"You have a fine gift for this, daughter," my father said, and kissed my forehead. I couldn't remember when he had last shown me such affection. But our work was not yet finished.

One of the ewes bled so heavily that I couldn't stop the flow, and I watched helplessly as the breath slowly left her. I held her lambkin against my breast and felt its own small heart racing with life. I wrapped it in a sack, carried it to the warmth of the cottage hearth, and fed it with the finger of a glove dipped in warm cow's milk. Then I fell exhausted onto my pallet, the orphaned lamb beside me, as the soot-black sky began to lighten.

The weather was mild for late March, the early morning bathed in a soft mist, and my father decided to turn the ewes and their lambs out into the pasture. It was a mistake. Later in the day, Tolly brought in the bloody, mangled body of a new lamb.

"Fox," he said, "or badger." I turned away, hoping it was not one that I had helped to birth.

Soon we heard one of the ewes bleating mournfully, unable to find her lambkin. "Where's the orphan?" Tolly asked. "Bring it to the barn."

Tolly had removed the skin from the dead lamb and showed me how to wrap my motherless lamb in it. I offered the little one to the grieving ewe, who sniffed the skin and was fooled into accepting the orphan as her own.

Just before darkness fell, Joan returned with Tom and Joan Little, bringing the glad news that her sister's child had survived and seemed to have gained some strength.

My stepmother had other news for us: She herself was once again expecting a child. "October," she said.

"Thanks be to God," said my father, touching her shoulder, and went out to see to his sheep.

❧

In late spring, soon after the tender green sprouts appeared, I enlisted Catty's help to weed the flax field— barefooted so as not to damage the delicate plants. In another month the flax was in bloom, and by mid-July the plants stood as high as my waist, ripe to be pulled, dried, retted, scutched, and spun. By late September I had a number of bobbins wound with linen thread, ready for the weaver's shop.

Stratford-upon-Avon had more than a score of weavers, but my father insisted that I patronize his friend, John Richardson. A visit to his shop might have been a pleasure, had it not been for John's son, Stephen, a loutish fellow who had forced an unwanted kiss upon me at a Twelfth Night celebration two years earlier.

Stephen's arms and legs were skinny as saplings, his wide-mouthed grin foolish as an infant's. I might have overlooked his appearance if he'd shown the smallest amount of wit, but it was evident he had none. I took pains to avoid him.

"Good morrow, Mistress Hathaway!" crowed my tormentor, advancing from the rear of the shop.

I hastily emptied my two baskets of spun flax on the table. "The usual weave, if't please you!" I called, fleeing toward the door. In ten days I would return to pick up the bolt of finished cloth, barely in time to prepare new linens for the babe Joan expected in less than a month.

My stepmother had asked me to stop by the herb shop of Wise Bessie to obtain a nettle tonic that promised to strengthen her womb. "It feels so heavy," Joan had complained, "as though the babe wants to come into the world before its time." I was bound for Wise Bessie's just as the pupils from the King's New School in Chapel Lane were released from their morning lessons. I spied Mary Shakespeare with Will at her side amid the boisterous crowd of schoolboys.

"Will is a pupil in the grammar school now," she explained as I fell into step with them, and Will chimed in, "I'm studying Latin—the eight parts of speech and the nouns and verbs. Would you like to hear my declensions?"

His mother smiled proudly. "My son takes in knowledge as the earth soaks up rain after a drought," she said.

Will rattled off a number of words, nonsensical to me, not stopping until we had arrived by the Shakespeare home in Henley Street. "We'd be pleased to have you join us for our dinner," Mary said, offering her warm and welcoming smile. Little Will had his say as well: "Aye, prithee, do come, Mistress Hathaway!"

I hesitated, thinking that I would soon be expected at home, but I was also tempted. *How much more pleasant this would be!* Mary laid a reassuring hand on my arm. "I know that Will would be made happy to spend a little time with you," she said, "before he returns to his lessons."

I yielded to the temptation and accepted, and I was soon surrounded by the Shakespeare family. The youngest, Anne, lay in the family cradle. When the infant grasped my finger with her tiny fist, I remembered how poorly my stepmother had looked when I left her in the morning. "Mind you don't tarry," Joan had said. But I *had* tarried, and now I could think of no way to leave without seeming rude.

Seated at the head of the table, John Shakespeare gave thanks. A maidservant served generous portions of meat and a finer type of bread than we Hathaways enjoyed. During the meal John asked about the well-being of our flocks, and Mary continued her inquiries about my family.

"My stepmother is soon to be delivered of another child," I said, feeling a qualm of guilt.

At the end of the meal, I thanked my hosts, promised to carry Mary's kind wishes to Joan, and agreed to escort Will back to his schoolroom. Skipping by my side, Will chattered about his Latin lessons—he had moved on to conjugating verbs. Once he had run to join his schoolmates, I rushed to the herbalist's shop and waited impatiently while Wise Bessie prepared the tinctures.

I knew from the ringing of the Guild Hall bell that several hours had passed since I'd left home, and hurried toward Shottery with Bessie's physicks in my willow basket. I recognized the rolling gait of Goody Winslow, the midwife, approaching along the field path from the opposite direction.

"Where have you been, Agnes Hathaway?" she asked sharply.

"Leaving off the flax to be woven for the new babe's swaddling," I said, adding uneasily, "and fetching a tincture for Stepmother at Wise Bessie's."

"No need for tinctures or swaddling now," the midwife said brusquely. "The infant came early and lived but a few minutes. I baptized him, as is my duty in such cases. They've been wondering what became of you." She glared at me.

My hand flew to my lips. "Oh!" I cried, and ran past

her, though it was too late and I should have been there all along.

Two days later I stood by the graveside. *If I hadn't tarried, if Joan had received the nettle tonic in time, would this child have lived?* To assuage my guilty feelings, I plaited together three prickly blackberry branches and with bloodied hands laid the thorny braid on the grave, calling upon the power of the Holy Trinity to fend off evil spirits intent upon snatching the soul of the dead infant.

The following spring, my stepmother was again with child. After the loss of her newborn, Joan became more determined than ever to protect her children from witches and demons. She hung hagstones over the pallets of Joan Little and Tom. She marked crosses on the doors with lime, nailed a phial of salt to the doorpost, and kept a pair of scissors, open to form a cross, under the cradle to ward off fairies. I suspected that she also bought certain charms from an ancient crone who lived near her old home in Drayton.

Her efforts seemed to be successful. At Yuletide my stepmother was delivered of a healthy daughter. The infant was christened Margaret, and we called her Meg.

CHAPTER THREE
• Simon Walford •

Y THE age of sixteen I had grown into a comely lass with hair the color of wheat, a narrow waist, a generous bosom, thick-lashed blue eyes set wide apart, good teeth, sweet breath, and a clear complexion. But my prickly discontent had deepened. Whether to blame that upon my own nature or the hostility of my stepmother, I cannot say.

On the feast of St. George, the twenty-third of April in 1573, the earl of Worcester's company of players, dressed in brilliant red cloaks and caps, swaggered into Stratford-upon-Avon, hauling their play-clothes and properties in a brightly painted cart. Announced by trumpets and drums, Worcester's Men had come to perform a masque in honor of England's patron saint.

Three or four times a year companies of players passed through Stratford. The troupes were usually invited to stop for a day or two to present their plays in the innyards. Townspeople as well as country folk from distant hamlets crowded into the courtyard of the Swan, the largest of several inns by the Clopton Bridge.

I enjoyed these performances whenever I had the chance, though my stepmother had nothing but ill to say of players and their plays. Players suffered from a sorry reputation and were beaten and jailed unless they traveled under the patronage of a member of the nobility. "Naught but a band of vagabonds, deserving of a whipping," she grumbled. But she did not refuse to let me go, and I persuaded my friend Emma Sandells to go, too.

A plump and lively girl with a heart-shaped face and a sweet disposition, Emma was her parents' youngest child. One after another her older brothers and sisters had married and gone off to establish homes of their own. Emma was the only one still living on the farm.

"Best to be born somewhere in the middle," she had sighed one day as we gathered cress from the brook. "I know 'tis a heavy burden when you're the eldest daughter, like you, Agnes," she said, piling another handful of the bitter greens into her basket. "But so it is also for the youngest, when the others have gone and your parents fear being left alone in their old age. Especially if your mother's constitution is not strong." Martha Sandells was often in poor health and needed Emma to look after her.

Emma and I spent as much time as we could together. To help his neighbors, my father had enlarged our flax field to supply the Sandellses' needs as well as our own. When Emma could leave her mother, she came to help me with the flax. While we worked, we often talked about our dreams for the future. Emma knew exactly what she wanted: a loyal husband, a cottage full of healthy children, a comfortable farm—just what her older sisters had, and her parents, too.

"That's what everyone wants, isn't it, Agnes?" she asked. "A home and family? What else could there be?"

"I don't know," I said. "But sometimes I think there must be something else—something different from what is expected of me." I didn't confess, even to my closest friend, how restless and unhappy I felt. "Sometimes I think 'twould be better not to marry," I ventured, "but to live alone with a garden and a cow and a few hens for company."

Emma stopped her work to stare at me. "What are you saying, Agnes?" she asked. "'Tis not possible for a woman to remain unwed! You'd likely be taken for a witch. It could end badly for you."

"Aye, I know that," I admitted. "But that doesn't stop me from thinking on it at times."

"You'll change your mind soon enough," Emma said with smug certainty. "The day you meet the right man."

"Mayhap," I said, shrugging. Emma was probably correct—but who was *the right man*? And where was I likely to meet him?

❧

Once Emma's mother had given her leave to watch the masque, we hurried to town, arriving at the Swan Inn ahead of most of the crowd and finding places near the makeshift stage. Will Shakespeare, who turned nine on that very day, was already there, seated on a bench with Gilbert and their father. John Shakespeare, who had long served as Stratford's official ale-taster, had recently been elected to the high office of chief alderman—head of the town council—and was entitled to the best seats. And he would determine how much the players should be paid, depending on how pleasing he found their performance.

Had it been up to me, I would have given every shilling in the town coffers to Worcester's Men, for I was immediately drawn to the player in the role of the dragon. Outfitted in doublet and hose of vivid green, his head covered by an enormous dragon's head of papiermâché with a great mouth revealing rows of fearsome teeth and a flame-red tongue, the dragon put up a fierce fight against St. George with his sword and coat of mail. Though we felt honor-bound to cheer for our patron saint, a goodly number of us believed the dragon had for once got the better of St. George.

After the masque had ended, the audience dispersed to the riverbank to continue the revelries. The dragon removed his disguise to reveal a thatch of thick blond hair, sleepy hazel eyes, and a strong cleft chin.

"Emma," I whispered, "let us go to meet the dragon!"

She readily agreed. We slipped through the crowd and stuck close to him until he noticed us.

His name was Simon Walford, and he told us he'd left his apprenticeship as a butcher in Upton Snodsbury to join Worcester's Men. I was powerfully attracted to the handsome player. Unfortunately, so was Emma. For a time Simon divided his attentions between the two of us.

When the music started, Simon bowed over Emma's hand. "May I have the honor, Mistress Emma?" he asked. Emma dimpled and blushed and accepted his invitation, dancing away and leaving me behind. John Shakespeare and his sons, strolling by the bench where I waited restlessly, stopped to pass the time of day with me. That was pleasant, but it didn't lessen my annoyance that the player had chosen Emma.

When Simon and Emma returned at the end of the dance, the two of us questioned him about his life as a player until the music began again. This time it was *my* hand he bowed over. *How well he dances!* I thought as we whirled away. I hoped that someone would come along to dance with Emma, whose turn it was to sit alone, but no one did. Even before the music stopped, Simon clasped my hand in his. "Come with me," he said.

I resisted, but not much, and off we went to sit among the reeds by the Clopton Bridge, leaving Emma to gape after us. I suffered a twinge of regret for deserting her. Emma would surely be angry—she had a right to be—but she would surely forgive me. Wouldn't she have done the same if Simon had chosen her? And wouldn't I have forgiven her? But I forgot all about Emma when Simon circled my waist with his strong arms and proposed that we have a kiss for each of the fourteen arches of the stone bridge that crossed the Avon.

I had been kissed only once before—by the oafish Stephen Richardson at Twelfth Night—a kiss as wet and soft as an overripe plum. Simon's kisses were nothing like that. Believing we were concealed by the reeds, I threw myself into this game with enthusiasm. The game ended when the church bells rang for vespers and I realized that

I was long since expected at home. I leaped to my feet, brushing grass from my skirts. Still breathless from our kissing I asked Simon, "When will you come back?"

"Whenever I can," replied Simon. He picked up a smooth stone from the riverbank, polished it on his sleeve, and offered it to me. "I promise," he said with a smile, and hurried away to find his fellows, who had drifted off to the inn for a pot or two of ale.

Emma was nowhere to be seen. I dropped the stone in my pocket and started for Hewlands.

I soon learned that Emma had reached home and sobbed out her disappointment to her mother, who passed the story on to her father, who then made a full report to *my* father of my behavior that afternoon. Much displeased, my father was waiting for me when I arrived at home. A generally mild-tempered man, he expressed his displeasure on this occasion with harsh words.

"I've long given thought to your future to ensure that you will one day have a suitable husband," he roared. "And I'd nearly reached an agreement with my friend, John Richardson, who has expressed interest in marrying you to his son when you're both of age and ready for such a step. But you complicate matters by running off into the bulrushes with the first player who catches your eye! What sort of life do you think you'd have with the likes of *him*?" my father demanded.

"A merry one," I replied, pertly and unwisely, remembering Simon's hazel eyes and warm kisses, "which is more than I can say about a life with Stephen Richardson." I knew that my father favored Stephen because his father, the weaver, was known as a shrewd tradesman. But surely Stephen was not *the right man*.

"The wench deserves a whipping for her impertinence!" cried Joan, who had been listening, her face flushed with the effort of keeping silent.

"I'll decide that," my father growled, and Joan, furious now, growled back at him, "'Tis unlikely that you'll do what any fool can see needs doing with this baggage." She jabbed her thumb in my direction.

While they argued, I saw my chance and slipped quietly away.

Later, when his anger had cooled, my father called me to him. "You know I would not force you to wed a man who is distasteful to you," he said. "But, when the time comes, I urge you not to turn away a good husband because his looks are less than pleasing. Think hard on it, Agnes. You could do worse."

At sixteen, of course, I was in no wise ready to think of a husband, but, when it came to that, surely I deserved one blessed with good looks as well as wit and humor. I placed the polished stone in a wooden coffer my father had once made for me, my initials AH carved on the lid.

And then I went to find Emma. "Forgive me, Emma," I said. "I've wronged you. I should not have gone off with Simon and left you alone."

Emma lowered her eyes. "And I should not have spoken of it to my mother. Have you been punished?"

"Nay," I assured her. "Not this time, though if Joan had her way I would have been."

Then we embraced and promised never again to be false to each other.

Season followed upon season, and in the autumn of 1574 when my brother Tom turned five, my stepmother decided that he should have an education. She urged my father to enroll him at a petty school in Stratford to learn his letters, after which he could apply for admission to the King's New School. The only cost would be for supplies, such as candles, ink, pen and paper, and a small amount levied for fuel to heat the schoolroom. Joan named off other boys who were pupils there: Will Shakespeare and his younger brother, Gilbert; Dick Field, the tanner's son; the mercer's two boys; and several more of her acquaintance.

My father was not convinced that sending Tom to school was anything other than a waste of time. "What needs the lad for an education in books?" he argued. "I could use his help on the farm, and if he wants to learn a trade, he can be apprenticed when he's fourteen."

But my stepmother held her ground until my father relented. Happy for any excuse to be away from the house, I agreed to escort Tom to his lessons in Church Street each day in time for him to be at his bench and ready for prayers by six o'clock on a summer morning, seven o'clock in winter. Tom would take his midday meal in town with Joan's sister, Alys, and I was to fetch him home again at six in the evening when lessons ended.

It was still dark when Tom and I knelt for our father's blessing and set off for town. Though I had no interest myself in education, the manner in which Tom learned to read pricked my curiosity. He had a hornbook, a sheet of parchment printed with the letters of the alphabet, framed in wood, and covered with an overlay of transparent horn. During our travels to and fro, Tom explained how letters could be paired to represent sounds. I found the process tedious, yet I began to learn.

Also printed on the hornbook was the Lord's Prayer, at first appearing to me like only so many marks on the page. Slowly I began to recognize simple words like *as it is in,* though it was some time before I could make out longer words like *Heaven* and *Kingdom* and *Temptation*. Even more puzzling was *Trefpaffes,* until Tom explained that an *s* in the middle of a word looked like an *f.*

"But why?" I asked. "It makes no sense."

He shrugged. "Doesn't need to make sense. It just *is.*"

At the age of eighteen, I believed reading was a skill for which I had no earthly use. At first I stayed with it to help Tom, but as the months went by I began to enjoy it. My lessons in reading came to be one of the true pleasures in my life.

CHAPTER FOUR
·The Queen's Visit·

HROUGHOUT THE spring of 1575 planning for Queen Elizabeth's summer progress through Warwickshire was the talk of Stratford. One bright morning late in June as I was closing my market stall, the eleven o'clock bell having rung in the stone-towered Guild Hall, boys from the King's New School trooped past, heading home for the Thursday half-holiday. Among them, as always, was Will Shakespeare, swinging his satchel of books. He usually passed on by with a wave, but that day he stopped to speak to me.

"Good morrow, Mistress Hathaway!" he sang out. Will was tall for his eleven years and slender, with a head of unruly tawny curls, a high, fine brow, dark eyes brimming with good humor and intelligence, and a winning smile. "Have you heard the news? The queen is coming!"

"I'faith, I have," I replied. "And I've high hopes that I shall go to see her." I'd suggested several times to my father that we all go, but my stepmother had opposed the idea, as she had most of my suggestions.

Will stepped closer and curiously examined the amber honey I was packing in my basket. "The queen and her court are to lodge at Kenilworth Castle," he said. The ancient castle was the magnificent home of the queen's favorite courtier, Robert Dudley, earl of Leicester. "They're to stay for nineteen days. I'm sure my father will be invited to one of the banquets in honor of the queen. If he's invited, mayhap I shall be, too."

Just that morning I had watched as Alderman John Shakespeare was escorted in a procession led by a mace-bearer to the Guild Hall for his daily meeting with the town council. I could see why Will might believe all that ceremony entitled his father to an invitation to a royal banquet.

Will rubbed his smooth chin thoughtfully. "And if I'm invited to dine with the queen, then I must learn to behave like a highborn gentleman in the presence of highborn ladies. To bow low, like this"—he doffed his schoolboy's cap and swept me a deep bow—"and to kiss a lady's hand, like this!" He dropped to one knee and, catching me off guard, seized my hand and kissed my fingers, sticky with honey. Nimble as a cat, he leaped to his feet and dashed off, calling over his shoulder, "High time you began practicing your curtsies, Mistress Hathaway!"

I laughed, thinking, *What a charming lad!* and finished closing my stall.

That evening I again proposed to my father that our family make the day's journey to Kenilworth Castle to see the queen. My brothers and sisters cheered the idea. This time Father persuaded Joan that it was something we must do and agreed to make the necessary plans.

For days my twelve-year-old sister Catty and I talked of little else. None of us could resist the gossip that swirled round the earl of Leicester, "the queen's most *favorite* favorite," according to Emma, who had happened by on a bright morning as Catty helped me drape our freshly washed linens over the hedges to bleach in the sun.

We'd all heard the story that Elizabeth had been in love with Robin Dudley when both were young, before she was queen, but his father had arranged Robin's marriage to Amy Robsart.

"I wonder if she loves him still," Emma mused, "and that's why she's never married."

"They say Leicester's poor wife died of a broken neck after a tumble down the stairs," I reminded her and shook out another wet sheet. "Rumor has it that he pushed her. But even if he's innocent, the queen can't marry him now, no matter how much she wants to. It wouldn't look right, now would it?"

"But that was long ago!" Emma insisted. "People say *he* still wants to marry *her*, and that's why he's spent ninety thousand pounds on special lodgings for her at his castle, to gain her favor!"

Gossiping about the queen and her court occupied us until every hedge was draped in sheets. "Tell me this," I said. "If the queen can remain unwed, why can't we all? Wouldn't we have a merry time of it without husbands to look after?"

Emma and Catty both stared at me, amazed at my peculiar question. "Why, 'tis the way of the world to marry!" Emma said at last.

I granted that she was right. But at that time in my life, marriage was a distant prospect, of no concern to me.

❧

Word reached Stratford-upon-Avon that Queen Elizabeth, accompanied by her vast retinue, was expected to arrive at Leicester's castle on Saturday, the ninth of July, after a stay in Coventry, a market town to the north. At dawn Tolly hitched our draft horse, Beau, to our wooden farm cart. Joan and the younger children made themselves comfortable in the bed of straw, and, dressed in our Sunday clothes, we began the fifteen-mile journey to Kenilworth. Emma's mother was unable to make the trip, and so Emma came with us. Father rode his favorite horse, Copper, sometimes changing places with Tolly, who drove the cart.

In celebration of such a rare event, hundreds of people thronged the deeply rutted road leading north, eager for a glimpse of our queen. Following the River Avon, we passed by Charlecote, the estate belonging to Sir Thomas Lucy, the wealthiest gentleman in our part of Warwickshire. At midmorning we swung wide of Warwick Castle, its mighty stone towers mirrored in the river's calm surface. By early afternoon we had joined the crowds in the meadows surrounding Kenilworth and found a place for our cart and horses near the narrow bridge that the queen's procession must cross. We settled down to wait.

The mood was festive. Jugglers in gaudy, tight-fitting clothes wandered through the crowd. The younger children heard rumors of a dancing bear and raced off to find it. Emma and I passed the time by weaving wreaths of bright marigolds growing nearby.

Many people had brought gifts to present to Her

Majesty. On each post of the bridge railing were displayed offerings supposedly sent down by the gods of ancient myth: wine, flowers, fruit, grain, even beautifully made tabors and pipes. I, too, had a special gift for the queen. Our lavender field was in full bloom, and I'd bought a ha'penny's worth of pale satin ribbon to weave through the stems and flowers to fashion a fragrant wand. I had worked for days to make something worthy of Her Majesty, having cast aside two that were less than perfect, but I hadn't yet thought how I would manage to present my gift to her.

The sun had wheeled nearly its full arc across the sky when the distant blare of trumpets announced the approach of the royal procession. I climbed onto the cart seat, straining for a sight of the queen. The excited murmur of the crowd grew louder, finally reaching a roar: "She's coming! She's coming!"

The crowd surged forward. I hadn't realized there would be such an enormous, jostling throng. Now, recognizing that I stood no chance of getting near enough to present my gift, I was close to tears. The lavender wand would certainly be lost in the disorderly heaps that now lined the roadside.

At that moment Will Shakespeare popped up by our cart in search of Gilbert. "Why so downcast, Mistress Hathaway?" he asked, noting my disappointment. When

I'd explained, he said, "Give me your wand. I'll deliver it to the queen myself."

Though Will was just eleven, he was blessed with a rare confidence. He had a persuasive appeal, and despite my doubts he could accomplish what seemed impossible, I handed over the beribboned wand. He darted off with it, weaving nimbly through the crowd. I tried to keep my eye on Will's cap but soon lost sight of him.

Suddenly green and white Tudor pennants fluttered in the light breeze and Queen Elizabeth herself appeared. For her arrival at Kenilworth, she was carried in a splendid litter borne by a half dozen strapping guardsmen handsomely outfitted in the Tudor livery. Gowned in yellow satin adorned with hundreds of sparkling jewels, her red-gold hair ablaze round her pale face, the queen smiled and waved to the cheering crowd. More jewels flashed on her thin fingers. People close to the roadway thrust their gifts out to her and held up their infants, so that when these children were grown they could say that they, too, had once seen their queen.

As the guardsmen marched smartly across the bridge with the queen's litter on their shoulders, a tall, wiry boy with tawny curls— *Will Shakespeare!*—suddenly leaped onto the railing.

"Look, Emma!" I gasped, pointing. "'Tis Will! He must be mad!"

Balancing like an acrobat, Will leaned far out and tossed the lavender wand so that it dropped neatly onto the queen's lap. He was promptly knocked off the railing and into the brook by the queen's guards, but not before she'd turned toward him, holding aloft the sweet-smelling wand like a scepter as her litter-bearers swept through the gatehouse and onto the castle grounds.

Will hobbled back to our cart, soaked and muddy, his hands scraped and bleeding, his doublet and breeches and hose torn, his cap missing, but nevertheless grinning jubilantly.

"Will," I said, "I am so grateful. I heartily thank you."

He pretended to doff his missing cap and made me another low bow, the sort a player makes to acknowledge the applause of the audience.

"William Shakespeare, at your service, fair lady," he said.

Emma clapped, and I blew Will a kiss.

❦

Hours later, swept along in a tide of hundreds of spectators, we were carried past the tiltyard to the shores of the Great Mere, an artificial lake formed by damming the brook.

"Come along with us!" Will called. "Gilbert and I will find the best vantage point for viewing the pageantry."

Emma and I, with Catty between us, followed the brothers through the crowd. The sun had set, drenching the pale sky with vivid streaks of peach and purple. Will pointed toward the lake where a torchlit boat appeared, decorated to resemble a sea creature. A singer with a harp sat astride the creature's back. Musicians hidden inside the boat accompanied the singer, whose deep voice floated over the shimmering surface of the dark water.

"That's supposed to be Arion, a poet from Corinth, singing and playing the lyre," Will explained. "Arion was the best singer in the world. The boat represents the dolphin that rescued him from the sea when he'd been thrown overboard by pirates."

Emma and I turned to stare at Will. "How do you know all that?" she asked.

"I read about it in some lines by the Roman poet Ovid," he replied, adding, "Ovid is my favorite poet."

Emma glanced at me and raised her eyebrows. *What a clever boy!* I thought, as proud as though he were my own brother.

The darkness deepened to a velvety black, a sound like a thunderclap echoed over the lake, and a shower of stars danced across the heavens. "Ahhh," the crowd sighed, thrilled. The fireworks continued, every display more brilliant than the last. The crowd sent up a cheer as each dazzling burst of light bloomed in the midnight sky, and Will reached for my hand and squeezed it.

❧

Before sunset on Monday our family returned to Shottery. The queen remained at Kenilworth for eighteen more days. I would have liked to stay on for the planned amusements, but my stepmother was heavy with the child she expected in a few weeks and could not be persuaded. The Shakespeares were among those who lingered; Will later told me that the queen was entertained with more fireworks, feasting and dancing, hunting parties, torchlight parades, and bearbaiting in which fierce mastiffs fought a dozen Russian bears to the bloody death of dog or bear, a sport the queen was known to enjoy.

"My father's gift of a pair of gloves, made of finest kidskin, was well received by the queen," Will said, but he made no mention of any invitations to a royal banquet, nor did I ask.

The gossips at the Thursday market talked of the queen's visit long after she had returned to London: "I hear that Leicester spent more than a thousand pounds a day to feed and entertain Queen Elizabeth and her retinue!" "They say that Leicester has again advanced his suit, imploring the queen to marry him!" "Has she accepted?" "Nay, they say she has once again refused him." "Mayhap another time."

We were left with a brilliant memory of our magnificent queen, and our lives returned to humdrum. I passed my nineteenth birthday; yet another year went by.

Then trouble came for Emma. Or mayhap she went looking for it.

CHAPTER FIVE
•The Bawdy Court•

MMA AND I were both at an age—twenty—when we yearned for a bit of excitement.

She found it first, at the Mop Fair. The fair was held each autumn at the end of the agricultural year, when debts were paid and workers hired for the new season. Fulke Sandells, needing a shepherd, talked with several men wearing tufts of wool fastened to their caps and soon struck a bargain with a young shepherd named Rafe, who agreed to live at Fulke's farm and look after his flock.

Rafe had scarcely moved his few belongings into a hut near the sheepfold than sparks began to fly between him and Emma. I met him just once—a tall, rawboned fellow with a ready laugh—and it was clear that Emma was besotted with him. I have no idea what his intentions were toward her, but I do know that only a short time later Fulke discovered them together in the barn and flew into a righteous rage. The frightened shepherd fled to who-knows-where, and Emma fled to Hewlands, searching for me.

She found me collecting the last of the season's honey from the hives. I draped her in a thin muslin veil to protect her from the bees and listened as she poured out her sad tale amidst a torrent of tears. "Oh, Agnes!" she sobbed. "My heart is forever broken!"

"What's broken can oft be mended," I said, as though I had experience in such matters, and added what consoling words I could think of.

"Not only that, but my father reported me to the Bishop's Council. His own daughter! Oh, Agnes," she wailed, "he's sending me to the bawdy court!"

I was stunned by this news. I knew that Fulke tolerated no nonsense of any sort, but this official church body dealt very harshly with immoral behavior. It would not go easily for Emma.

Soon after our conversation, her father hired another shepherd, named Francis, as old and gnarled as an oak, and kept Emma in strict seclusion. As further punishment she was forbidden to speak to me or even to send me a message, and so I would have no word from her until after she'd appeared before the court. All I could do was worry about the trial she faced while being unsettled by the knowledge that I had barely escaped the same fate.

Once the trial was over, we managed to steal a little time together when her father had gone to Stratford. "It was dreadful!" Emma cried. "I hope you never have to go through anything like it! Three men in black robes sat scowling behind a long table. They treated me like a wanton trollop, even though I swore to them that I was innocent of any wrongdoing, that I was not guilty of immoral acts. I wept and said I was dreadfully sorry for anything and everything I had ever done that might be considered a sin. I fell on my knees and begged their forgiveness. But they refused to believe me. No one believes me! And they've assigned me a terrible penance."

"I believe you, dear Emma, truly I do," I said. I put my arms round her and rocked her gently, like a child. "Soon this ordeal will be over, and you'll be happy again."

But first she had to suffer her penance.

Poor Emma! I was with my family among the worshippers at Holy Trinity on the Sunday that Emma was made to appear, dressed in a white sheet, barefoot and bareheaded, carrying a white rod. She was forced to stand before the congregation and publicly confess her sins. Her humiliation was awful to witness. When a member of the Bishop's Council ordered her to repeat what she had said so that God might hear every word, I couldn't bear to look at her and buried my face in my hands.

I was still shaking as we made our way home afterward. "Got what she deserved, the jade," my stepmother observed smugly.

"No one deserves such torment!" I snapped. "What gives a handful of old men the right to make a young woman suffer for a few innocent kisses?"

"Innocent, were they?" Joan laughed cruelly. "That's all *you* know."

"More than you do!" I retorted, louder than I'd intended.

"Quiet, both of you!" my father exclaimed. "This is the Lord's day, and you're raucous as a pair of crows."

Joan and I both fell silent, but I considered myself the victor, for it was rare for my father to speak so sharply to Joan.

During the week following Emma's penance, I crept across Shottery Brook in search of my friend, hoping to comfort her. But Fulke Sandells caught me and sent me away. "Let this be a lesson to you, Agnes Hathaway," he warned, shaking his finger in my face. "Best you mind your own behavior."

Picking my way back across the wet stepping-stones,

I considered how lucky I was that I had not been summoned by the bawdy court for my fourteen kisses by the Clopton Bridge with Simon Walford. And I vowed that I would maintain my virtue, no matter how greatly I might be tempted.

❧

My virtuous intentions lasted through the long and dreary winter—an easy matter, for there were no temptations. Spring lambing season enlarged our flock, my father sowed fields of barley and planted a flax field, and my stepmother uncovered her strawberry plants.

When sheepshearing time arrived in mid-June, my father hired sheepshearers from Alveston, a village east of Stratford-upon-Avon. They were men known in our shire to be quick and careful in their work. The day before the shearers were to come, Tolly built a dam across Shottery Brook to form a pool. Father drove the sheep into the water, and our shepherd, Thomas Whittington, plunged in up to his waist, washed the sheep with strong lye soap, and herded his charges upstream. With Tolly urging them, the sheep scrambled up the banks and into a pen, where they dried off in the warm sun.

The master-shearer and four others arrived soon after daybreak and set to work. A shearer dragged a sheep from the pen and, with a twist of his arm, flung the frightened creature down on its back. *Snip snip snip* went the shears, beginning at the head, until the fleece fell away in one piece and the near-naked sheep leaped off to join the flock. It was my duty to rush in and gather up the thick cloud of fleece and carry it off before the shearer seized another sheep.

All morning I observed a certain young shearer at his work. The sleeves of his smock rolled above his elbows revealed well-muscled arms. None cut closer to the flesh of the animal than he, and yet he never once nicked the skin. He must have sensed that I was watching him, for each time he went for the next sheep, our eyes met. He was tall and well proportioned. His easy smile displayed white teeth with no gaps, his nose was shapely, his ears did not stick out from his head, his eyes were clear and not too close together, his beard well trimmed. His brown hair, lightened by the sun, curled over his collar.

At midday Catty and I carried out table boards and trestles from the hall and set them up under the hawthorn trees. Joan had baked gammon pies and roasted several fowl, and there was plenty of ale to quench the thirst. I was keenly aware that the young shearer's eyes had been upon me as I laid out the meal. When I sat down in a patch of shade, he came and stood by me, holding his trencher of food.

"Christopher Swallow, called Kit, from Tiddington,

near Alveston," he announced in a voice both mellow and pleasing.

I told him my name as well and suggested he sit down and rest himself, which he did, and we both fell to eating. After a time I asked, "Have you a family in Tiddington?"

"Aye, a widowed mother, a younger sister, and none else."

"Where will you go when you leave here?" I asked, striving for conversation, and he answered, "To Fulke Sandells." I confess I already knew this, for I had agreed to help Emma.

"And then whence?"

Kit shrugged. "'Tis up to the master-shearer."

"And when the sheepshearing season is at an end?"

"'Tis haying season, and then time to harvest the barley. When the crops are in, I'll work some with a maltster in my village. In autumn as well as spring there's always plowing and planting and farmers in need of help. In June the wool will be thick again on the sheep, and 'tis likely I'll be back here next summer. Shall you be here, Agnes, when I come again?"

"'Tis likely," I replied with a glad smile.

Then Tolly called the shearers back to the sheep. This ended our exchange but began my fanciful notions, which entertained me during the long hot afternoon.

———

At the end of the day I was on my way home from Fulke Sandells's, where I'd been sent to borrow a salve for a sheep too closely clipped by a careless shearer, when I saw the men making their way down to the brook to wash themselves of the day's heat and grime. I stopped where I was and stood motionless as Kit stripped off his smock and knelt on the bank. He splashed water over his head and face, his arms and brawny chest. His body gleamed in the slanting rays of the sun. When he'd dried off, he took a clean smock from his bundle and combed his fingers through his wet hair.

I delivered the salve to Tolly, then hurried to the cottage to help Catty and Joan Little lay out a supper for the men. Though I wanted to continue my talk with Kit, I didn't want to draw the attention of my parents and the others—especially Joan Little. Her ten-year-old's face often puckered with disapproval and her glinty eyes seemed to miss nothing. I dared not exchange so much as a word or even a glance with Kit.

The shearers slept that night in our barn. I tossed upon my pallet in the hall, kept awake by visions of Kit Swallow's ready smile and naked shoulders.

❧

Shortly after sunrise the next morning I set out again for Fulke's farm. Emma was glad for my help, but she caught me gazing at the young sheepshearer and instantly guessed the meaning.

"Next you'll be in the reeds with him, sharing a kiss for each sheep he's sheared," she teased.

"Nay, not I," I retorted, too quickly, for such tempting thoughts had already crept into my mind. "I've no wish to find myself summoned to the bawdy court!"

"'Tis unkind of you to speak of it," Emma said, a little offended, though she had started it. "But he's a fine-looking fellow, I'll grant you," she admitted. "Have you learned anything about him?"

"He's from Tiddington, with a mother and sister there. Beyond that, I know nothing."

"Mayhap you'll learn more at the sheepshearing festival," Emma suggested. "We're holding it in our barn when the last of the shearing is done."

Our Cotswold sheep were among the best wool-producers in the shire. Fulke and my father had called upon their friend, John Shakespeare, to buy the thick fleece. Though John was trained as a whittawer, skilled in preparing kid and other fine skins for making gloves, he also dealt as a brogger, buying up wool from the farmers and selling it to weavers as far away as Birmingham and Coventry. It was suspected that he operated without the proper government license, but John had a reputation for dealing fairly with both farmers and weavers, and no one complained.

But they worried when they learned that after serving years as an alderman, John had stopped attending town council meetings. Gossip began to fly that John had fallen deeply into debt, forced to sell off his wife's inheritance, including her family's property in Wilmcote. My father would have offered to help out his old friend, but my stepmother was unsympathetic to John Shakespeare's problems.

"He's brought it all upon himself," she said sourly. "'Pride goeth before destruction, and an haughty spirit before a fall,'" she added. Joan was fond of quoting scriptures when they suited her purposes.

Nevertheless, on the day the shearing was finished, John came by and made his offer. My father and Fulke were well satisfied at the price, and they all shook hands on it.

❧

That night—shearing finished, accounts settled—we celebrated with a festival. Musicians played tabors, pipes, and bagpipes for dancing. Singers sang pretty ballads, poets mounted stumps to read their works, high-leaping morris men in red breeches danced with bells on their knees and ankles. There was an abundance of food and drink for all.

Among those who came out from town for the merry-making were John Shakespeare, displaying no outward sign of worry, and his wife and children. Will boldly pulled me into a spirited dance with three other mismatched couples.

"Your sweetheart?" Kit teased me later.

"Mayhap," I replied with a playful smile, "when he grows up."

And he *was* growing up. I saw Will often at church and at the market, but it still surprised me that the clever little boy was now a loose-limbed thirteen-year-old already taller than I was.

It was well past the midnight hour when the last of the celebrants drank up the last of the ale and stumbled toward home. The musicians had long since been paid and wandered off. A peaceful silence fell over the darkened cottages. Animals, young children, and old people slept.

But not Kit, nor I. Kit would soon be leaving, and for the past hours he had never been far from my side. Despite my earlier resolve, I had ignored Emma's knowing winks and the malevolent stares of Joan Little. Hand in hand we wandered down to the brook, where a bright moon spilled silvery coins upon the rippling water. Kit drew me close and pressed his lips upon mine, lingering until I finally remembered my determination to maintain my virtue and pulled away.

"Don't forget me," I whispered.

"Nay, I shan't forget you, Agnes," he called softly after me as I started toward the cottage. "I'll come back."

That was just what Simon Walford had said.

❧

But Kit was true to his word. Within weeks, when haying began, he came asking for work. And my father, who had looked favorably upon Kit as a sheepshearer, hired him. Kit's presence for four days of haying proved a delicious torment. It was my pleasant duty to carry refreshments out to him and the other laborers at midmorning and again at dinnertime. I stayed as long as I could to watch the ripple of Kit's smooth muscles and the rhythm of his swinging scythe.

But I had plenty of work of my own: The garden needed tending; the brewing of ale continued apace, requiring my trips to town twice each week; and Thursday was another market day. Wanting to stay at home for once but unable to find an excuse not to take my honey and bunches of lavender to sell, I dragged my feet on the walk to Stratford and fairly flew on the way home a few hours later.

From sunrise until sunset the men toiled in the field, scything the hay, turning and raking it into windrows. They stopped only to eat and drink and to snatch a few minutes of rest with their broad-brimmed hats pulled over their faces. In these brief moments Kit and I managed to exchange a few whispered words.

We had been blessed with fine weather, so that by the time the last of the hay had been sheaved, the first was ready to be heaped on staddle-stones that kept rats out of the hayrick. But now the skies were lowering, and we rushed to get the crop under cover. On the last day the laborers collected their wages and prepared to be on their way.

I was gathering eggs when Kit, his bundle on his back, came to the garth. "Will you walk with me a while, Agnes?" he asked. I set down my basket and followed him.

Once across Shottery Brook, Kit pulled me off the path and into a grove of trees, where we eagerly made up for some of the kisses we'd missed and I gave only a fleeting thought to my resolve. As we continued at a leisurely pace in the direction of Tiddington, still several miles distant, a fine mist began to fall. We paid no attention. Tiny droplets collected on Kit's silky beard. I wiped them away. Stopping occasionally for a kiss or two, we didn't notice that the sky had darkened to an angry purplish black, until suddenly the clouds burst open, unleashing a downpour. We dashed for shelter in a nearby barn and sprawled there, laughing and breathless.

While we waited for the rain to stop, Kit told me about his mother, long a widow; and his sister Margery, born with a crippled leg; and about his father, killed when a tree fell upon him while he was employed by Sir Thomas Lucy to build his mansion at Charlecote, not far from Kit's home.

Sir Thomas was well-known in Warwickshire. The Lucy family attended services at Holy Trinity each Sunday, parading down the aisle of the church as though sent by God Himself. Knighted by the queen, he held the office of high sheriff and justice of the peace, a man feared as much as he was respected. Sir Thomas had used his wife's fortune to build the mansion.

"Sir Thomas cared nothing for our plight," Kit said, his face turning dark and resentful. "He cared not at all that my father lay without speaking for a fortnight before he died, leaving my mother with me, still of an age to wear a russet dress, and Margery, not yet out of swaddling."

"Do you work for Sir Thomas now?" I asked. "Surely 'tis time to forgive him."

"Nay, I'll do no work for him, and I'll not forgive him. With all his wealth he might have helped us, and he did not. Ofttimes we went hungry. But he maintains a warren at Charlecote that teems with game, not just coneys but red and fallow deer as well. Were it not for the game, there have been many days when we would not have had a morsel of food on our table."

"You poach, then?" I asked, alarmed. Penalties were severe for stealing game from private property.

"Aye, I take a deer or two each year and a brace of rabbits as we have need of them. I've not been caught yet, though there's been many a near miss with his gamekeepers."

"'Tis dangerous, Kit," I said. "It would go badly for you if you were caught."

Kit smiled. "Don't worry about me," he said. "I can take care of myself."

The rain had stopped. Kit still had miles to go, and I would surely be missed at home. Kit kissed me one more time, a pledge to return in August for the barley harvest. Then he went on toward his village, and I hurried back toward Hewlands, inventing a story as I went of having been with Emma when the rainstorm began and sheltering in the Sandellses' barn until it ended.

And I managed to convince myself that my virtue had not been spoiled by a few harmless kisses.

CHAPTER SIX
•*Gloves*•

NCE BARLEY ripens, it must be brought in quickly, before it sheds its seed. It is not cut with a scythe, like hay, but with a serrated sickle held in one hand, the rough-edged stalks of barley grasped in the other. It was customary for the farmer to make each hired man a gift of a sturdy pair of gloves at the beginning of the harvest. Father sent me to John Shakespeare's shop to buy them.

Behind a wooden counter that had been lowered outside the glover's shop window, Will was arranging a display of lambskin gloves, deerskin bags, and an assortment of belts, breeches, and sword-hangers. Nearby lay a stack of the three-fingered cowhide harvesting gloves.

I had not seen Will since the sheepshearing festival,

but I'd heard that his life had changed abruptly: He had withdrawn from the King's New School.

My brother Tom, now a pupil in the lower school, understood what a loss that must have meant to Will. "The upper school boys hear their lectures in Latin, and they read, write, and speak in Latin. They study ancient history and memorize the works of Roman poets. The boys all say that Will was the best pupil," Tom reported. "The headmaster believed he'd go on to study at the university."

Yet here he was, at his father's shop, greeting me in his usual cheery manner as though nothing had happened. "Good morrow, Mistress Hathaway!"

"Good morrow, Will," I replied, and hesitated—would it be cruel to ask him about school? But Will saved me from embarrassment.

"You've doubtless heard the news—I'm becoming a glover, but one who speaks Latin with great fluency," he said. He rearranged some of the display so that a pair of pretty lambskin gloves caught my eye. "My father wishes me to leave the schoolroom for the larger world and become like him, both artisan and tradesman, maker and seller. But I haven't altogether left the great Latin poets—especially my favorite, Ovid. The headmaster has granted me the use of his library."

No one I knew talked like Will, except the vicar at

Holy Trinity in his Sunday morning homilies. Will described the skill he was acquiring in his father's work as whittawer, learning to dress the skins of animals to be made into gloves. "I now know how to make sizing for the skins—the smell is worse than the sulfurs of hell!— and to cure them with salt and alum. I hang them to dry in the shed behind the workshop, and shave them with paring knives. Hence these wounds of battle." He held out his hands, showing me the cuts and scrapes.

"All this and more is to be mastered before my father will consent to teach me the glover's skills of cutting and stitching. There's much to learn about glove-making— more even than the conjugations of Latin verbs! Mayhap by the queen's next visit I'll have a pair ready, and surely you'll make her another pretty lavender wand."

"Then we must think of a better way to present our gifts," I suggested, remembering his tumble into the brook at Kenilworth.

Will replied with an amiable smile, "Aye, we must. But this is not why you've come. 'Tis harvesting gloves you're after."

While he pointed out their specific qualities—the toughness of the leather, the evenness of the linen stitches, the reasonable price—my attention was drawn to a single pair of beautifully wrought gloves made of cheverel, the finest kidskin. My father kept a small herd of goats, and his best—and only—customer for cheverel was John Shakespeare. I examined the gloves, undoubtedly from one of our herd, and decided to try them on. The delicate gloves fit perfectly, but they were priced far beyond what I could afford. Besides, I had no need of such a luxury, ill-suited to my linsey-woolsey smock and my ordinary life.

"I haven't the money to buy them," I told Will, putting them back.

"One day I shall make you a pair," he promised. "But before I do, Father says I must learn to choose the skins. Soon I'll visit Hewlands to look over your young kids. Just think of how innocent they are of their future!"

"As we all are," I murmured, counting the coins for several pairs of the harvesters' gloves into Will's open palm. When I glanced up, our eyes met. How intense his were! I was the first to look away.

A sound from inside the shop drew his attention. "By your leave," he said, turning to go. "I'll call at Hewlands within the fortnight, Anne. Will you be as pleased to see me then as I shall be to see you?"

How bold! I thought. The lad was only thirteen, and I was within days of my twenty-first birthday. Had he forgotten his manners completely, addressing me not as "Mistress Hathaway," but as "Anne"? And why *Anne* and not *Agnes,* the name given me at my christening, the name by which I was called? The two are similar, the one sometimes changed for the other; by whose leave had this boy made the change?

But I was so caught up with my growing feelings for Kit Swallow and the prospect of seeing him again soon that the matter of Will's impertinence quickly slipped from mind.

❦

The flax was ready to be pulled, and Emma crossed the brook to help me. I was glad of her company, for Emma loved to talk, and her prattle made the work go faster. She was in love again, this time with a thatcher named Robin Whatley. She had met him when her father decided to put a new roof on his cottage. Now it was "Robin says this" and "Robin believes that" as we jerked the plants up by the roots and threw them into piles.

We worked under a sun so hot that Emma had removed first her petticoat and then her bodice until she was working in her shift. I soon did the same. We had no thought that anyone might observe us in our state of undress, until I heard someone whistling—and looked up to see Will Shakespeare at the edge of the flax field. "Anne!" he called. "Shall I come help you?"

"Zounds!" Emma muttered. "What impudence! Tell him to go away."

"Wait for me in the garth!" I shouted, scrambling for my clothes.

Emma stared after him as he sauntered off. "I think our young glover has eyes for you, *Anne,*" she said. "And since when have you been called by that name?"

"'Tis some strange notion of his," I said, lacing my bodice. "He's here to buy kidskin. I'll tend to him, and then I'll be back."

Hens and chicks and a few ducks surrounded Will in the garth, and an ill-tempered goose honked at him. "I've not come to see your poultry," he said, shooing away a strutting red cockerel. "'Tis the goats that interest me."

"Aye, that I know," I said, irritably, and led the way to the enclosure where the young kids were kept.

The kids were Catty's responsibility. She cared for them as lovingly as a mother cares for her infants. To assure that their skins remained as soft as rose petals, she fed them only milk and would not allow them to browse among the pasturage. Keeping them in an enclosure, surrounded by soft bedding, protected their delicate skins from bruising and scratching.

Catty became so attached to her charges that she shed tears when the time came for Tolly to slaughter them for their perfect pale skins and for the tender veal that I would sell at a good price at the market. She could hardly bear to part with them, and she might even have refused to talk to Will about them.

"Sir Thomas Lucy has ordered a half dozen pairs of cheverel gloves as a gift for Lady Lucy," Will explained. He knelt among the gamboling kids and examined each one with care.

Lady Lucy flaunted her wealth. Her capes and hoods were lined in scarlet, and she wore the brilliant silks and bright satins permitted to gentlefolk but denied people of lower birth. Now she was to have not one pair, but a half dozen pairs of fine gloves, and, as it later turned out, another half dozen for their daughter, a rude slip of a girl as haughty as her mother. I was tempted to tell Will about the death of Kit's father and how poorly Sir Thomas had treated the Swallow family, but I thought better of it. Everyone knew of Lucy's cruelty and influence. John Shakespeare no doubt needed Lucy's business.

Will decided to purchase all six of our kids. "I'll come back to pick up the skins when they're ready," he said, gazing at me more intently than I thought the transaction warranted. "You look lovely today, Mistress Hathaway," he said, a lilt in his voice. "Lovely as a summer's day," he added.

I felt the blood rising to my face. "Why do you call me Anne?" I asked with a frown. "No one else does."

"I like the sound of it, 'tis simple as that. Pay attention to the sounds of words, of names, of places. There's pleasure in it for the ear, *Anne*."

Unable to think of a reply, I turned away, wanting to return to Emma and the flax field. Will caught my hand. "Hold a moment, Anne. I wish to talk to you."

I jerked my hand away. "What is it you wish to talk about?"

"Many things. Poetry, for one."

"*Poetry?* I know nothing of it."

"Then mayhap I could teach you. Walk with me."

"I have work to finish," I protested. "Emma's waiting."

"Only as far as the field path," Will coaxed.

"But no farther," I said. I was curious, so I agreed.

Will talked, and I listened. "I won't spend my life as a glover, you see. I'm doing this now because my father needs me. But that will end someday."

"And then how *will* you spend your life, Will?"

"As a poet."

"A poet?" I repeated, laughing. "Surely you jest!"

"Aye, a poet," he said, and I saw that he was in earnest. "And mayhap a player as well. Better to write the spoken words than to be the one who speaks them. Best of all, though, to do both."

We had reached the path through a field of barley, and I stopped. Will broke off a few stalks of ripening grain, idly plaiting them together as he spoke. He tied the ends to make a loop, and, reaching for my hand, slipped it onto my wrist like a bracelet. "Someday you'll see, Anne. And now, fare thee well!" Off he darted, light and quick as a dragonfly.

I hurried back to Hewlands, scarcely knowing what to make of the conversation, or of my own behavior. Why was I bothering at all with this youngster?

Emma, who had fallen asleep under a hawthorn tree, awoke. "What became of you?" she demanded sullenly. "I've nearly finished pulling the flax." Then she examined my face. "Your cheeks are scarlet, but from shame or some other cause, I can't say."

"From running. I got into conversation with Will, and next I knew, I'd walked partway to town with him."

Emma noticed the woven bracelet on my wrist and clucked her tongue. "Have you taken leave of your senses, Agnes? Will Shakespeare is an *infant*!"

"Aye, but fast becoming a man." I dropped the bracelet in my pocket.

"You need someone who is already a man, not one who is *becoming* one. Kit Swallow, for one."

"Aye, Emma, I know that," I said. "Kit will soon be here for the harvest."

Later, when we'd hung the flax on a rack to dry, I

placed the straw bracelet in my wooden coffer for safe-keeping.

❧

When Kit arrived for the third time, he received a hearty welcome at Hewlands. I found him appealing in every way: handsome, of kindly disposition and good humor, apparently honest, and able to make me laugh. Tolly liked him. My father admired the hard work he gave in exchange for food, drink, and a day's wages. His easy manner won the younger children, with the exception of Joan Little, who could not be won by anyone. Only she and her mother found fault with Kit.

"Sly, that's what he is," Joan grumbled. "All those false smiles! I trust him not."

Kit's long hours in the field meant that our times alone together had to be snatched after the others had retired for the night. It had been a long time since Emma had been punished by the bawdy court, and I no longer gave any thought to my vow of virtue when I crept out of the cottage and ran to the barn to meet him after everyone was sleeping. During those sweet hours I lay encircled in his arms, his warm breath upon my cheek, and his lips close to mine. We spoke in low voices, about everything and nothing, until the stars began to fade and I had to creep back to the cottage, leaving Kit to steal what rest he could before the day's work began. But he was young and strong, and the loss of sleep scarcely bothered him.

When the last of the barley sheaves had been carried to the barn, I grew melancholy at the thought of his leaving. "You won't stay for the threshing?" I asked hopefully.

"Nay, there's others to do that. But don't fret, Agnes," Kit said as we murmured tender farewells. "We'll not be long parted. Your father has spoken of hiring me to help with the late plowing and sowing the winter crops. I'll be back before the snow flies."

The weeks of autumn passed, colder and wetter than usual. The threshers arrived, flailing the grain on the barn floor to separate the seed from the husk. With a damp handkerchief tied over my nose and mouth I helped with the winnowing, pouring the grain from a basket held above my head to a sheet spread on the floor. Catty stood by, waving a straw fan, and a breeze blowing through the open doors carried away the chaff. After a while we changed places. It was hard, dirty work, and at the end of the day our arms ached painfully.

Joan was again expecting a child. She was no longer young, and each pregnancy took a greater toll on her. She complained of sour stomach, aching back, headache, sleeplessness. Her temper was shorter. She hadn't the strength to chase me or Catty round kitchen and buttery with a wooden spoon, as she once had, but she was more sharp-tongued than ever. Nothing I did suited her—I did everything too quickly or not quickly enough—and we exchanged many bitter words.

Catty, the youngest of my mother's children, had grown to be a shy and winsome girl of fourteen years. Bless her, she was devoted to looking after Joan's children, which now included John, called Jack, born soon after the queen's visit to Kenilworth. But Catty didn't get along much better than I did with our stepmother. Once after she had been denied food and drink for an entire day as punishment for some small misdeed, I'd smuggled her a cup of ale and a bit of stale oatcake, as Tolly more than once had done for me. Catty gobbled down the food and then laid her head in my lap, begging, "Tell me about our mother, Agnes. You remember her, surely?"

"Aye, I remember her," I whispered. I held my sister and gently stroked her face, swollen and wet with tears. "She was a good soul, and she loved you dearly."

"I wish she were with us still," Catty murmured in a voice choked with sadness.

"I do as well, but we mustn't question God's will. He has sent us Joan Little, and Tom, and Meg, and Jack, and soon another will join us," I reminded her. "And you do love the little ones, that's plain."

"Aye, but were our mother still alive there would surely be other little ones to love, and her to love us, too."

"In a few years' time," I whispered, "you will have husband and children and a home of your own, and all will be well."

We fell silent, each of us lost in our own thoughts. But even as I comforted my sister, my own longing deepened painfully. *When will* my *life change?* I wondered. *How much longer must I bear it? When will all be well for me, too?*

❧

The rains finally stopped. Once the ground had dried out sufficiently, Kit was hired by neighboring farmers not only for plowing fields and planting wheat but also for helping with such work as slaughtering pigs and cleaning out the cesspits beneath the privies.

Kit shirked none of it, no matter how unpleasant, and often found work in the neighborhood of Shottery. When he did, he always came to visit me. If one of Kit's employers sent him to Stratford-upon-Avon on an errand on market day, we managed to meet on the riverbank near the Clopton Bridge to share a few furtive kisses, though I was always mindful of prying eyes eager

·82·

to report us to the bawdy court. But by December it had grown too cold for such outdoor exchanges of affection, and even our heated caresses couldn't keep us warm.

"I'll be back at Twelfth Night," Kit promised, drawing his finger gently along the line of my chin. "We'll dance again, dear Agnes, and kiss the whole night through."

I loved the dancing, and I cherished the kisses, but I had begun to realize dancing and kissing weren't enough. I wanted more. I counted the days and dared to hope that Kit Swallow might be *the right man,* the one who would someday soon change my life.

CHAPTER SEVEN
• *St. Stephen's Day* •

S YULETIDE approached, Catty and I took our sister Meg to gather holly and ivy and other greens to deck the hall. Joan, who spent much of the day resting by the hearth and issuing orders, grudgingly turned over much of the cookery to me. It became my task to prepare most of our meals; Joan usually disliked whatever I made and shoved aside her trencher with a curled lip. "If you should ever be so fortunate as to find a husband," she complained beyond my father's hearing, "you will likely poison him with your cookery."

"Men have strong constitutions," I replied. "Else Father and Tolly would have long since expired." *From your efforts, not mine,* I thought, but didn't say.

With Catty's help I prepared a Christmas feast: roast mutton, turnips and cheese, prune pies, frumenty—a wheaten pudding flavored with honey and cinnamon—and many other dishes. On this occasion I went about the task with a glad heart. But Joan found fault with nearly all of it. Only thoughts of Kit Swallow and his promised return on Twelfth Night kept me from sinking into melancholy. Emma and I made plans to meet with our sweethearts at the Twelfth Night party in Stratford.

On St. Stephen's, the day after Christmas, I wrapped myself in my woolen cloak and started out to the barn to milk the cows. Hoarfrost crackled beneath my feet, but I stopped to listen when I thought I heard the low whistle that was Kit's signal. I echoed the whistle and listened again. Had he come back sooner than he'd planned? When I was certain it was Kit, I ran to the byre at the end of the barn where cows and horses were stalled during the winter. Kit was there.

My joy at seeing him before he was expected quickly turned to dismay. He was dressed only in breeches and smock—no jerkin or cloak—and shivered with cold so that his teeth were chattering. His smock was torn and spotted with blood.

"Kit!" I gasped. "What happened?"

"Lucy caught me," Kit replied through cracked and swollen lips.

"Caught you?" I repeated.

"Taking a deer."

I understood at once. "You were poaching."

"Aye, Agnes, I was." Kit with his wounded mouth had difficulty speaking as he explained what had happened. "My sister has fallen ill, and I'd given my mother every tuppence I had left from my earnings to buy them a cow. They were short of food, and so I helped myself to one of Charlecote's herd of fallow deer. A good-sized doe it was, and she would have fed them for months. Lucy had me whipped and would have thrown me into prison if I hadn't managed to escape. Now I must flee."

"Flee? But, Kit, where will you go?"

"North to Yorkshire," he said. "I know of a cousin there who raises sheep. I mean to find him and ask for work."

"Yorkshire!" I exclaimed. "'Tis a far, far distance! When will you ever come back?" I clapped my hand over my mouth. Tears pricked my eyes.

"That's just it, Agnes—I can't come back here. Sir Thomas made it plain that I was fortunate to get off with a few stripes on my back and six months in prison, and he swore that an even greater punishment awaits me if he sees my face again."

I rushed into Kit's arms, weeping. He held me close and whispered into my hair, "I know I ought not ask it of you, but I dare to beg it of you, dear Agnes. Come away with me!"

"Come away with you?" I drew back and gazed up into his eyes. I cared for Kit, but was I ready to run off with him? I didn't know. A rush of sentiment pulled me first one way, then another. Part of me wanted to follow my heart: *Go with him! This is your chance to get away!* But another part of me urged caution.

"Where would we live? What would we do?" I managed to ask. I felt confused, bewildered, and I wanted him to make plain what he was asking of me.

"I'll find work with my cousin, and we—you and I—can find a croft in which to live. Once settled, I'll send for my mother and my sister. Oh, do say you'll come!" he pleaded. But he hadn't said the words I needed to hear: *I love you, Agnes. Be my wife.*

"Is it that you don't care for me?" he asked when he saw my hesitation.

"Aye, I do care for you, Kit, and deeply." For a long moment I kept silent, struggling with my feelings. My life at Hewlands under the heavy fist of my stepmother was far from happy. *If you should ever be so fortunate as to find a husband,* she'd said, her voice dripping venom. Her ill-tempered daughter, Joan Little, was becoming more vexing with each day. Kit was offering the escape I'd been waiting for. Mayhap he would soon speak of marriage. Mayhap another chance would not come for me. I closed my eyes, praying that when I opened them again I would see my way clearly.

I opened my eyes, and though the world still seemed blurred, I said, "I'll come with you, Kit," and sealed my decision with a kiss.

❦

Kit needed a place to hide while I made my preparations. Though my father was no friend of Sir Thomas, Lucy was a powerful man in the region who demanded respect and allegiance. As high sheriff he meted out harsh justice, especially to anyone bold enough to steal game from his property. As much as my father liked and admired Kit, I was sure he would not willingly defy Sir Thomas, or harbor the thief who had tried to rob the man and now was running away. It was important to keep Kit well hidden from my father as well as from anyone who might come looking for him.

I told Kit to stay in the byre and promised to return soon with whatever spare clothing I could lay hands on.

"And mayhap a bite to eat as well?" he asked. "I've had nothing since yesterday."

"All you could want," I promised.

Our crowded household was noisy and bustling, as usual. Seeing that Joan Little was occupied with tormenting Meg's gray kitten, I was able to accomplish my errands unnoticed—except by Catty, who eyed me as I prepared to carry two large bundles to the byre. "What are you doing?" she asked suspiciously.

I didn't want to lie to Catty, but neither could I tell her the whole truth, and so I settled on a half-truth. "Kit is hiding in the byre. Sir Thomas caught him poaching deer, and I'm helping him to escape."

But Catty seemed to guess that I hadn't told her everything. "Say that you aren't fleeing with him!" she begged. "I couldn't bear it if you left, Agnes!"

"Nay, dear Catty, I'm staying right here," I murmured, hoping she wouldn't look into my eyes and know that I had indeed lied.

Gratefully Kit dressed in the warm clothes I'd brought him—a worn doublet belonging to my father, an old cap and ragged cloak that Tolly was unlikely to miss. Kit devoured the portions of bread and meat I'd brought him as well as a flagon of ale as he outlined his plan for us.

"Try to sleep for a few hours, if you can. We must be well away by second cockcrow, long before first light. It wouldn't do for Sir Thomas's men to discover us on the road. Be sure to dress in several layers of clothing, for 'tis bound to be even colder as we travel north. Will it be hard for you to get away?"

I shook my head. "No one is likely to notice." I thought of Catty, alert to my mood, and shrewdly watchful Joan Little and prayed that I was right.

"Bring such food as you can. And a lantern, if possible."

I said I would.

"There's one more favor I must ask of you." Kit's mouth tightened. "I have no money. Not a farthing. Do you have a few coins that you might bring? We shall surely make use of them."

"Aye, I do—a little."

Kit pulled me close. "What a brave and lovely girl you are to do this, Agnes!" he said, but I felt my courage flagging even as he spoke of it until he kissed me—gently, with his wounded lips. "I'll whistle when 'tis time," he promised.

❦

Noses red, Tolly and Shepherd Thomas came into the cottage, stamping their feet and rubbing their hands. They'd been looking after the sheep huddled in the sheepfold but gave no sign of having noticed anything amiss in the byre.

After a supper of porridge, the family was early to bed, as usual. I lay upon my pallet next to Catty, listening to the wind howling round the chimney like a wild animal.

Once the breathing of the other sleepers was deep and regular, I stole out of bed and assembled my few possessions in a hempen bag, dressed in two woolen petticoats over a linen shift, and collected some bread and cheese, mutton, half a prune pie, and several apples from a barrel in the buttery. Lastly, I opened my wooden coffer and took from it a cambric handkerchief my mother had once given me and in which I'd tied a penny or two on market days, when I'd earned a bit extra from the sale of honey or beeswax or candles. The sum of the coins equaled a shilling and a few pence over. I lay down again upon my pallet, fully dressed, to await Kit's signal. Unable to sleep, I tossed restlessly, my mind tumbling first one way, then another, worry mingling with excitement.

I was leaving home, leaving with a man who said he wanted me by his side. How good it would be to get away from the querulous Joan, who carped at me from dawn to dusk! I would certainly not miss her. Nor would I miss the spiteful Joan Little, who at the age of eleven showed every sign of becoming even worse than her mother.

But then I thought of Catty. How could I leave my dear sister, abandoning her to our stepmother's endless faultfinding? And what of the younger ones—clever Tom, jolly Meg, sweet-tempered Jack? I'd grown fond of each of them, and they of me. In many ways I was like a mother to them. If I left them, would I ever be able to come back?

I wished I could talk to Tolly about it, but he was unlikely to understand. Tolly—steady, humorless, solid, honest—was nothing like Kit. Tolly would never steal a deer, I was certain. And what would he think of me, running off with Kit without the promise of marriage or even the mention of love? Mayhap Kit had come here only because he needed my help, and not because he truly loved me. But he *did* love me, didn't he?

If I intended to go, then I must do it quickly, before my doubts overcame me.

Without waiting for Kit's signal, I moved stealthily from under my blanket and gathered my bundles from their hiding place in the buttery. I picked up a lantern holding a tallow candle, and with a pair of tongs pulled a glowing ember from the banked fire and placed it in an earthenware saucer. Balancing these things, I stepped outside, softly shutting the door behind me.

All was quiet. Hoarfrost shone in the pale light of a large crescent moon. I took the long way round to the byre so that my footprints would not be readily noticed. Inside the barn I plunged into complete darkness. I blew on the ember until it glowed, lit the candle from it, secured the candle in the lantern socket, and by the dancing yellow light groped my way to the byre. Kit was asleep in an empty stall, half buried in straw. I set down the lantern, knelt close beside him, and waited, listening to the cows' drowsy shifting and Kit's own gentle breathing.

He awoke suddenly, apparently sensing my presence. "Agnes?" he whispered. "Is't you?"

"Aye," I answered. "'Tis."

Kit's hands were cold when he reached for me, but his mouth was warm. "Are you ready then?"

I said I was.

We silently left the barn, bowing our heads against a brutal wind that blasted steadily out of the north. Ice coated the stepping-stones across Shottery Brook. Once safely on the other side, I turned to look back once more at Hewlands Farm, the thatched cottage where my family slept on unaware, the barn with the byre and sheepfold where the animals dozed. I could barely see through my tears to follow the glow of the lantern Kit carried.

We walked quickly past the Sandellses' farm, where a dog began to bark. A lump rose in my throat. I'd not had time to bid farewell to Emma, my dearest friend, and I prayed that she would understand. The farther we walked, the heavier my heart grew. The cold settled into my bones.

We spoke little. After a time we approached the farmer's barn where Kit and I had once taken shelter from a summer storm. "May we rest here out of the teeth of the wind?" I pleaded. "Just for a little, to warm ourselves."

Kit looked at me carefully. "We can't stop for long," he said. "I wish to bid farewell to my mother and sister, and our croft lies too close for comfort to Charlecote. I won't rest easy until we're on the Coventry road and well beyond Lucy's grasp."

This barn proved no warmer than ours at Hewlands. Kit took my hands in his, chafed them, and blew his warm breath on them. I drew my hands away and began to cry.

"I cannot go any farther with you, Kit," I murmured through my tears.

"You cannot?" Kit sounded surprised. "Why not?"

"'Tis not the right thing for me to do," I said in as strong and steady a voice as I could muster. "My place is at home at Hewlands. 'Tis not right to leave like this. I must go back."

Kit was silent, rubbing his beard. "This is your decision, then?" he asked finally.

"Aye, 'tis."

He didn't argue or ask why I had changed my mind. I handed over the sack of provisions, and when he at first refused to take the coins I untied from the handkerchief, I persuaded him of the dangers he faced. "'Tis not much, but if you have no means at all, you will surely be taken for a vagabond and punished for it."

He nodded and dropped the coins into his bundle.

There seemed to be nothing more to say.

"I cannot change your mind, then, sweetheart?" Kit asked at last.

"Nay, Kit, you cannot."

"Then grant me one last request—a lock of your hair."

I consented. Kit removed his knife from the sheath on his belt, carefully cut a strand near my face, and tied it with a bit of thread torn from the hem of Tolly's cloak.

"Now give me one of yours," I said, and he did so.

We shared a last embrace, and Kit swore he would never forget me, the only promise he could make.

Tears blurred my last view of Kit Swallow when he turned to wave. The glow of the lantern grew smaller until it was only a winking jewel in the darkness. As thick clouds moved in to shutter the moon, I started toward home.

❧

Long before I reached Shottery Brook, I saw the flames. I dropped my bundle and broke into a run.

By the time I arrived, out of breath and sick with fear, tongues of fire were licking at the barn. My father and Shepherd Thomas were driving the terrified animals, bleating and squealing, away from the roaring fire and into the pasture. Joan crouched nearby, rocking and keening. Catty and Joan Little and our two maidservants, Lib and Maud, lugged leather buckets of water from the brook.

Tolly, his face streaked with soot, grabbed a bucket from one of the girls and heaved the water onto the fire. Suddenly the flames reached up hungrily and caught the thatched roof. Sparks leaped and shot up into the frosty air in an awesome display.

"What's happened?" I cried, unable to move. My feet seemed rooted to the frozen ground.

Tolly returned the empty bucket to Lib and snatched a full one from Maud. "Must have been someone in the byre with a candle or some such—a vagabond, likely. The straw caught. We've lost a greater part of the grain."

I gasped. *The ember in the saucer.* I'd blown on the coal until it glowed red again, touched the candlewick to it, and set the lighted candle inside the lantern. We'd hastened to collect our things and be off, leaving the ember, dead and turned to cold gray ash in the saucer. Or so I thought—if I thought at all. But the blustery wind must have forced open the barn door, no more than a finger-width but enough to let in a draft that sent a handful of straw dancing onto the ember, not dead but only sleeping.

My legs buckled and I fell down in a swoon. Catty rushed to my side, but Tolly dismissed her curtly. "Run to Fulke Sandells and bid him come. Francis, too, and any servants who are about. I fear the cottage may catch next." He dashed the bucket of water on the flames and stood over me, glaring down fiercely, his fists knotting and unknotting. "Where have you been, Agnes?" he demanded. "What do you know about this?"

Tolly turned without waiting for an answer and continued heaving water onto the fire, to no avail. I crawled away, sick at heart, unable to think what to do or say.

Fulke and Francis came running, snatching up buckets of water from the creek on their way, pitching the water on the voracious flames. Soon other neighbors, John Debdale and his son, Martin, arrived to help, still in their nightcaps.

It was useless. The flames would not be satisfied until they had taken it all, consuming the barn and moving on to the sheepfold as well.

My fault, my fault, my fault.

Catty crouched beside me. "Was it Kit?" she whispered.

I shook my head. "My fault," I said, weeping. "All my fault."

Joan Little stared at me, eyes narrowed and glinting. "I saw you, Agnes," she hissed. "I saw you take the ember from the hearth, and I saw you carry it out to the barn in a little dish. You did it on purpose," she finished smugly.

"Nay, nay!" I insisted. "It was a terrible accident!"

"I don't believe you," she taunted. "I think you're a witch."

"Whisht!" Catty exclaimed, jumping to her feet. "What a dreadful thing to say, Joan Little! Such remarks could be dangerous. Now take this bucket and fill it for Tolly, and let us hear no further such wicked talk from you."

CHAPTER EIGHT
•Twelfth Night•

HE BARN was destroyed, the grain crop lost, a cow and two pigs dead as well as the little pied pony used to deliver the jugs of ale. In my carelessness I had brought my family to near ruin. And Kit Swallow was gone and with him a chance to escape my unhappy life and start anew.

I can hardly begin to describe the depths of my despair in the first cruel days after Kit's flight and the devastation of the fire. I avoided Joan—and Joan Little, with her accusing stare and knowing smirk—as much as it was possible to avoid anyone. Tolly must have known I was somehow to blame, but he said nothing, and I don't believe that he implicated me to our father. Joan Little could be counted on to do that.

At first, Emma was the only person I could talk to. She tried to comfort me when I finally told her what I had done and how it had ended.

"You truly loved him then?" she asked.

"I don't know, Emma! In truth I scarcely knew him. And when it finally came to running away with him, I couldn't bring myself to do it. I only wish I had made my decision sooner—*before* I took the ember to light the lantern."

Days later I gathered my courage and admitted my guilt to Catty, not only for causing the fire but for lying to her about my intention to leave Kit.

Catty was silent for a time. "'Twas a terrible thing you did," she said at last.

"Aye, it was," I replied, tears beginning to course unchecked down my cheeks.

"But you are to be forgiven for it," she said and squeezed my hand. "I don't blame you for wanting to leave. I'm sure I would have left, if I had been in your place."

My sister continued, her tone now darkly bitter. "Stepmother despises me. She makes my life a misery. I can't bear it, and I don't know how you can! I still don't understand why you didn't leave when you had the chance," Catty said with a sigh. "But I'm so thankful you didn't."

Numbly I plodded through the remaining days of Yuletide. I could scarcely bring myself to look at the charred skeleton of the ruined barn. The embers still smoldered. Our neighbors had taken in our poor animals until the barn could be rebuilt, and twice each day I stepped across the frost-slick stones of Shottery Brook to Fulke Sandells's byre to milk our cows. Often Emma came to help me, once she'd finished her own milking. Once, coming home with a brimming pail in each hand, I lost my footing and plunged into the icy water, spilling most of the milk. Surely I deserved this wretchedness. But Emma didn't think so, and filled my pails with milk from her family's cows.

My responsibility for the fire continued to weigh heavily upon my conscience. A week after the barn had burned, I found my father alone in the midst of the blackened ruins, staring at the skeleton outlined against the somber gray sky. Dropping to my knees on the frozen ground I begged him to hear me out. He listened silently as I confessed the entire unhappy story, beginning with Kit's poaching, his beating and banishment, and ending with my change of heart and return in time to see the flames consuming the doomed barn.

My head bowed, I awaited whatever penalty he

would decide was just. He might strike me, send me away, give me some terrible but well-deserved penance. For a long while he was silent. Then, when I thought I couldn't bear the suspense any longer, he laid his hands on my shoulders. "Let us speak no more of this, daughter," he said. "I believe you've had punishment enough."

Gratefully I leaped to my feet, kissed my father, and gave my solemn word that I would never again disappoint him.

❧

I knew well the story of Twelfth Night, the eve of Epiphany: The three Magi, carrying gifts of gold, frankincense, and myrrh, followed a star to a stable in Bethlehem and found the infant Jesus, lying in a wooden trough and surrounded by shepherds and beasts of the field. Since my childhood that story had reminded me of Hewlands Farm. I liked to imagine such a wondrous event happening in our own barn with Shepherd Thomas Whittington and our cows and sheep as witnesses. But the barn was no more, and Kit, with whom I had weeks earlier expected to pass that Twelfth Night in dancing and kissing, was gone as well.

Joan's sister, Alys, and her husband, Samuel Fletcher, the carpenter, had invited our family to come to Stratford-upon-Avon for the festivities. But my stepmother was feeling unwell, and my father said he would stay at home with her and the two youngest children. Tolly, who was courting a girl from Tredington, a few miles south of Shottery on the River Stour, had ridden down to visit her.

Having no wish to answer the questions that would surely be asked about the fire, I would have stayed at home, too, if Catty had not persuaded me to abandon my somber mood for one evening and come along with her and Tom. Then, to my displeasure, Joan Little invited herself to join us. We set out for town, carrying torches to light our way over the snow-covered fields.

The streets of Stratford-upon-Avon were filled with merrymakers, many wearing such elaborate disguises that it was impossible to guess if they were male or female, young or old, peasant or gentry. Musicians roamed from house to house, playing bagpipes, flutes, and sackbuts. We made our way up Rother Street through the good-natured crowd, drawn by the sound of laughter that spilled out of Samuel's handsome half-timbered house.

Rosy-cheeked Alys Fletcher had laid a generous table in the oak-paneled hall with plum puddings, sweetmeats, and a great wassail bowl of lamb's wool, spiced ale in which floated roasted apples that had burst their skins and resembled snowy fleece. I threaded my way through the crowded hall, quickly becoming separated from Joan Little—a relief—but also from Catty and Tom. I nodded to those I recognized, many of them tradesmen: John Page, the ironmonger, and his two daughters; Richard Hornby, the smith, and his wife, Rachel; Henry Field, the tanner, his wife, Elizabeth, and their son, Dick; Rafe Boote, the button-maker, and many others besides, all drinking toasts with hearty cries of "Wassail!"

Finally I managed to push through the cross-passage and found myself in the buttery, where I stumbled upon several couples locked in passionate embrace. Among them were Emma and Robin.

Emma broke away from her lover and kissed me. "Agnes," she whispered excitedly, "Robin and I are to be handfasted at Candlemas. Will you come?"

"Aye, to be sure!" I cried, showing as much enthusiasm as I could for her betrothal and hoping the bawdy court didn't get wind of this amorous scene.

Emma returned to Robin, and I continued on to the kitchen. One of Samuel's apprentices was roasting apples for the wassail bowl while another basted a joint turning on a spit; sweat streamed from their brows. A maidservant was cracking nuts; others rushed in and out, exchanging empty platters for heaping ones. All were singing or talking loudly and shouting rude jokes. The din was terrific.

The boisterous merriment contrasted sharply with my state of mind. It would be much better to spend the evening at home—even in the company of my stepmother—than in the midst of such revelry! I began to work my way back through the hall, searching for Catty to tell her that I was leaving. But someone placed a steaming mug in my hand, and at that moment the entire Shakespeare family entered the hall: John and Mary; Will and his brother, Gilbert; their two sisters, Joan and Anne; even little Dicky. Holding the mug of ale, I waited for a chance to wish them the greetings of the season before I left.

I was attempting to make myself heard over a deafening burst of music when an ancient crone appeared suddenly at my side, nearly knocking me down. Rotund body buried in thick petticoats and shawls, head and face hidden beneath a bonnet and kerchief, the crone boldly snatched the mug out of my hand, drank down the contents, and half dragged me to the center of the hall that had been cleared for dancing.

I could not imagine who might be so heavily disguised, but the crone danced with ungainly enthusiasm. For a time I pretended to enter into the spirit of the occasion.

But then I began to wonder: Could this cavorting crone be Kit Swallow hidden beneath the bonnet and layers of petticoats? Would he have dared such a thing? The crone was surely no female; the height of my dancing partner, the manner in which he grasped my waist so familiarly—all persuaded me of that. I tried to examine the hands, but the crone wore gloves. I tried to look at his eyes, but the light was dim and the bonnet shielded them.

It must be Kit, I thought, my excitement growing; *Kit has come back!*

When he seized my hand and led me out of the noisy house to a dark and secluded spot in the rear garden, I followed willingly, eager to be swept up once more in Kit's warm embrace, to tell him all that had happened.

"Oh, I'm so glad—," I began, but I got no farther. The crone, whoever he was, pushed me against a rough stone wall, his mouth hard and wet against mine. His hand fumbled clumsily beneath my bodice.

With all my strength I shoved him away, tearing off his bonnet and kerchief. I gasped. It wasn't Kit Swallow. It was Stephen Richardson, the weaver's son. I choked back a wave of revulsion and spat onto the ground.

"Now, Agnes," he whined.

"Crackbrain!" I cried furiously. "Are you determined to learn nothing? Years ago you kissed me against my wishes on Twelfth Night, and now you've tried once more. I find you as loathsome now as ever I did then!

Do not ever, *ever* again touch me, or try to kiss me, or even to speak to me. Do you understand, Stephen?"

I rushed away from my tormentor, plunging back into the house from which music and laughter still poured. And I ran directly into Will Shakespeare.

"Ho!" cried Will. "So Mistress Hathaway has come to dance with me after all!" He peered at me closely, his smooth young brow creased with concern. "Does all go well with you, Anne? You look to be in some distress."

"I could do with a bit of lamb's wool, but I've misplaced my mug," I said, trying to calm myself. "Mayhap a dance later."

"Allow me to fetch you another," Will offered gallantly.

Will disappeared into the crowd as a trumpeter blew a fanfare and Samuel Fletcher called for silence. "The time has come to choose the King and Queen of Misrule," Alys announced, and pointed out two enormous Twelfth Night cakes displayed next to the wassail bowl.

The queen's cake, rich with butter and eggs, had a dried pea hidden in its depths; a single dried bean was buried somewhere inside the king's spiced cake. The man and woman who found the pea and the bean in their slice would rule over the evening's merrymaking. Two maidservants cut the cakes, while others passed out pieces to the guests.

Catty, flushed with excitement, joined me with two slivers of the queen's cake, one for each of us. I pushed aside the revolting memory of Stephen's slobbering mouth and groping paw, and dutifully bit into my portion. There was nothing in my slice.

But Catty's eyes widened. "Agnes," she whispered. "I found the pea." She showed it to me. "Here, you take it," she said. "We'll tell them 'tis yours. I don't want to do this."

"Of course you do, Catty!" I urged. "You're sure to enjoy it. Go on, now."

She hesitated until I prodded her again, and then she spoke up timidly. "Here 'tis. I have it."

A shout went up, and the crowd parted to make way for a young man blushing to the roots of his dark hair. My sister, likewise blushing, stepped forward to meet him. Alys Fletcher draped the royal couple in discarded grain sacks trimmed with scraps of fleece. Samuel set crowns made of bits of cloth and wood on their heads. The royal couple shyly joined hands as the crowd cheered.

"Who is our king?" I asked Will, who had returned with a mug of lamb's wool. "Do you know him?"

"Aye, 'tis Edward Stinchcomb, the new usher lately arrived from Oxford to teach at the lower school."

I recognized the name; Tom had spoken of him.

"I've heard that he's skilled in playing the lute," Will continued. "I'm thinking of hiring him for lessons."

The musicians, taking up their pipes and horns and tabors, began to play a lively tune for a jig, led by the newly crowned king and queen. Will took my hand. "And now, Anne Hathaway, the dance you promised me."

I abandoned all thoughts of leaving the party and stepped out with him.

❦

When the dance ended, Will suggested that we retreat from the uproar of the hall to the comparative calm of the kitchen. "Prithee, Anne," said Will, once we'd found a place to sit out of the way of the bustling servants, "tell me what put you in such an agitated state when I first saw you this evening."

I hadn't intended to speak about it, but Will had a way that coaxed the story out of me: my mistaking the crone for my "friend," Kit Swallow, and having the crone turn out to be the weaver's son, Stephen, who had behaved so boorishly.

"I know nothing at all of Kit Swallow," Will said, "but a great deal of Stephen Richardson. I would have thought him more snuffling milksop than cankerous varlet."

Snuffling milksop? Cankerous varlet? Will's words made me laugh. I hadn't laughed as much in some time, as I now did with him.

Will helped himself to a handful of sweetmeats from a passing platter and shared them with me. While we nibbled honeyed almonds, I asked him to tell me about his life as a glover.

"By day I do as I must," he said, "which is as my father wishes. By night I do as I like: I write my poems. My father thinks this a foolish pastime, but my mother buys me paper, ink, and quill and says nothing to my father of the expense."

"I've told you, I know naught about poetry."

"My poems are mere scratchings. Your red cockerel, his foot dipped in an inkpot and racing across paper in pursuit of his favorite hen, could write a better poem than I can even imagine. Though I do believe I'm improving."

"But on what subject are your scratchings, as you call them?"

"Love," he said. "Like the red cockerel after his hen, always of love."

You have only down upon your cheek! I thought. *What do you know of love?* But I held my tongue.

Then Gilbert burst in, and my brother Tom, followed by the two Shakespeare sisters and Will's friend, Dick Field. Will proposed that we sing a catch, a round for several voices, and started us off with "Hold Thy Peace." The Shakespeares all knew it, Tom and I learned speedily, and we sang with gusto. The tune was easy enough and the words equally simple:

> *Hold thy peace, and I prithee*
> *Hold thy peace, thou knave,*
> *Hold thy peace, thou knave, thou knave!*

Each time we repeated the refrain, *Thou knave,* our voices grew louder, until we were fairly shouting:

> *Thou knave! Thou knave!*

Our singing soon drew the attention of others, who came to join in. Dick Field introduced another song, "Hey Ho Nobody at Home," a catch for five voices. Still more people crowded into the kitchen, including the King and Queen of Misrule, my sister glowing with pleasure and her consort clearly uncomfortable in the role that had been thrust upon him but gamely attending her. Joan Shakespeare, a sweet-faced girl with a pert nose and light brown curls, coaxed Will into the hall to dance a boisterous trenchmore, while the rest of us stayed in the kitchen to continue the singing until they came back.

Nose, nose, nose, nose
And who gave thee that jolly red nose?
Cinnamon and ginger, nutmeg and cloves,
And that gave me my jolly red nose!

Someone, returning from a visit to the privy in the garden, noted that the third cock had already crowed and the sky begun to lighten. Catty laid aside her crown and royal robes and said good night to her king. I found Tom asleep in a corner and Joan Little spying upon a pair of lovers in the buttery. The four of us trudged wearily back to Hewlands through a pretty sprinkling of fresh snow. Everyone else was long abed.

I said my prayers, adding special thanks that no one had said anything to me about the fire after all, and lay down on the pallet I shared with Catty. She rolled onto her back and whispered drowsily, "Agnes, do you think I'm too young to fall in love?"

Remembering how smitten I'd been at sixteen when I met Simon Walford, I smiled in the darkness. Who could have stolen my sister's heart?

"How old are you now, dear Catty?" I asked, though I knew well the answer.

"Nearly fifteen."

"But not until April."

I thought back over the evening. Will Shakespeare, perhaps? Was it possible? Had they danced together? I couldn't remember. It seemed Will had spent much of the evening with me.

"May I ask, who is the object of your affections?" I asked.

"Ned," she whispered.

"Ned?" I searched my memory. "I don't know anyone of that name."

"Edward Stinchcomb, the King of Misrule," she said, a trifle irritated by my forgetfulness. "I found out that he teaches at the lower school. Oh, Agnes, he's so handsome! So kindly!"

"And so old," I observed drily.

"Twenty-four," she said. "Not so old."

"Too old for you, dear sister," I said. "He'll soon be looking for a wife, and you're far too young for that. Now may we sleep a little before we must be up and doing?"

CHAPTER NINE
· Handfasting ·

OR THE whole of January the sun remained smothered in a thick pall of dark and ominous clouds—day after day of iron-hard cold and unrelenting dreariness.

One bright spot in the long winter was the betrothal of Emma and Robin. On Candlemas, forty days after Christmas, several families from Shottery and a few close friends from Stratford gathered in Fulke's hall to witness the handfasting. The two fathers bound the couple's clasped hands with cords, and Emma and Robin looked into each other's eyes and pledged themselves to marry. The cords were untied, and Robin produced a pretty gold ring made in three parts: One he placed on Emma's right hand, one he took for himself, the third he gave to me, their witness, to keep until the wedding when the three parts would be united on Emma's ring finger.

After the ceremony the guests feasted on pigeon pies from George Whatley's dovecote, dried-apple tarts and perry cider from Fulke's orchards, and my stepmother's double ale. The Shakespeares were among the guests, and while the rest of the company ate and drank to the happiness of the betrothed couple, John drew my father aside and offered to lend him enough money to rebuild his barn. The first part of the loan would become due at sheepshearing, the balance with interest at Michaelmas, after the harvest was in and debts were settled. My father gratefully accepted the offer.

"Why would the man lend you money when he is in such hard circumstances himself?" Joan asked when my father told her of the arrangement.

"Because he knows that I will repay it as promised. 'Tis a good return on his money. John likes to do business with friends he can trust."

But my stepmother disliked John Shakespeare. She'd heard the rumor that he wished to be recognized as a gentleman and had applied to the College of Heralds in London for a coat of arms. She'd been gratified when he was turned down. More recently, she'd observed the

Shakespeares had been absent from church several weeks in a row. "Still practicing the old faith on the sly, I'll warrant," she had said more than once.

England had been a Catholic country during Queen Mary's reign. But Mary's successor, her sister Elizabeth, was Protestant and required her subjects to worship in the Protestant Church of England. Those who stayed away were fined a shilling for each absence. Everyone knew of families who complied with the law yet secretly followed the Catholic faith, though penalties could be harsh, including imprisonment and even death. My stepmother was especially wary of our Shottery neighbors, the Debdales, whose eldest son, Robert, had fled to France to become a Catholic priest.

But my father disagreed with Joan's suspicions of John Shakespeare. "More likely, John is simply discomfited by his financial problems."

"We shall see," Joan said smugly.

❧

Emma's handfasting prompted Joan to bring up once more the subject of my own future prospects. "You're not getting any younger," she reminded me as we sat knitting stockings by the hearth. "At one-and-twenty 'tis high time you put your mind to finding a husband. Another year or two and you'll be past your prime, fruit that's hung too long on the bough."

"I scarcely need reminding, Stepmother," I snapped, dropping a stitch.

I thought of Kit Swallow and wondered again if I had erred in turning back. Now my closest friend was betrothed, pledged to marry within the year, and would doubtless move to Temple Grafton, Robin's home. My brother Tolly was making frequent trips to Tredington to visit Isabella Hancocks, a sturdy girl with a practical manner. I happened to be present when she came with her father to negotiate the purchase of several sheep, and I think Tolly recognized at once that she would someday make him a good wife. He was not yet in a position to marry—a man was expected to have the means to support a family—but that time could not be far off. Selfishly, I dreaded Tolly's leaving, as I dreaded Emma's.

Joan would not let the subject alone. "There's no lack of suitable young men in Warwickshire," she insisted, wooden needles clicking steadily. "Other girls seem to find them—just look at Emma! The fault lies with *you*, Agnes. You want too much, and you think you deserve it."

"Too much?" I yanked angrily on the yarn, sending the ball rolling across the floor. "Is it too much to believe that I deserve a decent man who'll love and respect me?

You somehow managed to find such a man when you married my father, though Lord knows what *he* got in the bargain."

"Mind your wicked tongue, brazen hussy," Joan warned, needles clicking faster. "Even now you're more of a burden than a help."

Stung, I ignored the warning and plunged ahead. "I've never understood why my father married you. Mayhap he was willing to settle because his children were young and he needed a wife. But I'm not like my father. I have no cause to settle for third-rate goods." I fixed her with an icy glare as I spoke, so that she could not mistake my meaning.

I had gone too far. With an oath, my stepmother sprang from the settle, ripped the half-finished stocking from my hands, and flung it into the fire. The smell of burning wool filled the hall as she stalked out.

I understood that the words we'd spoken could not be unsaid, and whatever fragile tie that had existed between us could not be mended. And I cared not a whit.

❧

Winter made way for spring. The crusted snow shrank to patches of white against the dark earth, and a few early flowers—daffodil, primrose, flower-de-luce— bravely peeped through. The air softened and lost some of its bitter edge, and Samuel Fletcher arrived at Hewlands with several apprentices to build a new barn.

The men dragged away the charred timbers of the old barn and hauled down a number of elm trees from the ancient Forest of Arden to the north. My father sketched out the dimensions of the new barn on the damp ground with a sharpened stick. The apprentices trimmed the logs with an adze and set the heavy posts upright on stone to keep out dampness.

During the winter months, when the weather had allowed, Catty and I had taken the younger children to the riverbanks to gather willow sticks and hazel twigs, which we heaped in the lee of the cottage. Now, as the beams were being secured in place, Samuel showed us how to weave the sturdy sticks with limber twigs to form wattles, panels that would be fitted between the posts.

The youngest apprentices mixed straw and horsehair with dung and mud to be daubed thickly with a trowel over the wattles. Daubing took a certain amount of skill, but one of the apprentices undertook to teach me and refrained from laughing when the daub fell off almost as soon as I smeared it on. It was cold, hard, dirty work, but because I knew I was to blame for the loss of the barn, I forced myself to stay at it until my bones ached and my muscles throbbed.

During those long hours, my thoughts constantly

roamed in search of Kit. *What has become of him? Is he safe?* The road he intended to take would have brought him dangerously close to Charlecote. *What if Sir Thomas Lucy caught him when he went to visit his mother and sister? What if Lucy made good on his promise to throw him into prison? Would I even know?* These questions tormented me, and I had no way to find answers.

Emma sometimes came to check on our progress. Her real interest sparked when her beloved Robin arrived with the thatchers to put on the roof. Robin's job was to fasten the rafters to the ridgepole, forming the framework that would hold the bundles of reed thatching.

"I'll be glad when sheepshearing is over," Emma observed, gazing up at him as he worked.

"And why is that? 'Tis months away," I said. I turned to scoop up more daub and saw Emma dimple and blush.

"Robin and I plan to wed once the shearing is done. We'll live with my parents until after the harvest, so that Robin can help."

I was pleased to learn that Emma's marriage would not immediately take her away from Shottery, and despite my muddy hands and dirty apron, I threw my arms round my friend's neck and kissed her heartily on both cheeks.

While I continued to slop and smear, Emma entertained me with plans for her wedding.

"I'm to have a new petticoat and bodice," she said. "John Richardson is weaving a length of cloth from wool I've spun, and my mother has promised me indigo for dyeing it."

"Richardson!" I grumbled. "I'd rather wear the same old petticoats to my grave than set foot in that shop again."

Emma laughed. "Poor Stephen! You ought to take pity on him, Agnes. He seems like a decent fellow, and I think he pines for love of you."

"Decent? He's a *snuffling milksop*. A *cankerous varlet*!" I cried, quoting Will Shakespeare. "He'll not have my pity, or anything else from me," I said, slapping a trowelful of daub onto the wattle. This time it stuck.

"Dear Agnes," Emma said, throwing up her hands, "I didn't mean to upset you. Surely you must be lonely, and I only meant that he might provide you with welcome companionship."

"Aye," I confessed, "'tis true—sometimes I'm lonely. But never so lonely that the likes of Stephen Richardson will fill the empty place in my heart. I'd rather remain unwed and a virgin all my days than marry a man who does not truly love me with all his heart and soul."

"I pray God that you will soon find such a man," Emma said kindly, "for a woman without a husband is no woman at all."

No woman at all? If that was true, it was a sobering thought. But before I could discuss it with Emma, Robin climbed down from the rafters, and Emma's concern for me vanished in the wink of an eye.

Within a fortnight the thatching was complete, the wattle and daub finished, the barn ready. Under a thin and watery sun, with shepherd Thomas's guidance, we led the animals from their lodgings with hospitable neighbors—Fulke Sandells and John Debdale among them—to their new home in time for the lambing season.

❦

Joan's birthing pains began soon after supper on the night a late spring storm roared down from the north, driving before it snowflakes as big as pigeon feathers that quickly buried our familiar world. When Tolly set off for Stratford-upon-Avon to fetch Goody Winslow, the midwife, we could see no farther than the gate. Then the gate, too, disappeared.

As Joan's pains increased, so did our worry. Where were Tolly and the midwife? Catty stayed with Joan, doing what she could to ease her; I stayed away, knowing that my presence was no comfort. An hour passed, and then another, and another. I kept an anxious watch out the window, but there was no sign of my brother and Goody Winslow. The wind howled ominously round the chimney. My father paced and prayed and cursed himself: "I should have gone in Tolly's stead." Twice he put on his cloak, determined to go out in search of the missing ones, but each time Catty and I managed to dissuade him, arguing that we would then have one more to worry about.

It seemed from Catty's observations that the birth was imminent. I hoped that Joan, having given birth a half dozen times before, might deliver herself unaided, although she'd always had the help of a midwife. Yet time passed and the infant remained unborn. Hearing their mother's cries and moans, the younger children fretted. I tried unsuccessfully to calm them. Hard to bear were the malevolent stares and wicked mutterings of Joan Little. In the past weeks I had found various charms—bits of cloth with strange markings—under my pillow and in my shoes. I suspected they were her efforts to cast an evil spell upon me, though for what reason I could not imagine; perhaps she needed none.

Near midnight Catty came down from the upstairs chamber, distraught and wringing her hands. "She must have help," Catty said. "The babe won't come and she's worn out."

My father turned to me, his face ashen. "Go to her, Agnes. You can deliver her, just as you have the ewes. Your hands will know what to do."

"A woman is not a ewe," I protested. "And I don't believe she'll let me touch her." I was thinking of the harsh words we'd exchanged a few weeks earlier; we'd avoided each other and spoken as little as possible since then.

My father's eyes were pleading. "I pray you, Agnes, go to her. She has need of you."

Taking the rush candle, I climbed to the upper chamber. Joan lay on the bed, panting. Despite the cold, her face was bathed in sweat and her thin hair clung damply to her forehead. "Goody?" she asked weakly. "Is't you?"

"Goodwife Winslow cannot come because of the storm, Stepmother," I said, speaking quietly, soothingly. "But I'm here to help you." I set down the candle and, kneeling by the bed, took her hand in mine and gently chafed her bony fingers.

"Agnes? You?" she cried. Another pain wracked her, and in spite of herself she gripped my hand until it passed. "Not you," she said firmly. "You know even less of these matters than you do of any other." She cringed away from me.

"Nay," I said, "I know some things. I'm a woman with a woman's body. You must let me try. 'Tis the only way."

I called down to Catty, instructing her to warm some mutton broth and bring it to me, along with a dish of butter. I fed the strengthening broth to Joan, spoonful by spoonful. At last, with great reluctance, she allowed me to touch her in her most private places. My hands made slippery with butter, I assisted her, as I had the laboring ewes just days earlier. Father was right: My hands somehow knew how to ease the unborn babe into a better position, as they had the lambs.

"It will go easier now," I promised Joan, and it did. Within the hour, an infant boy had joined our family, mewling feebly.

My grateful father gave me the privilege of choosing a name for their new son.

"William," I said. "I've always liked the name."

In midmorning Tolly stumbled in, exhausted. He had lost his way in the storm, ridden in circles, and finally found shelter at a farmhouse in Drayton. Three days later we bundled the infant in sheepskin and carried him through rapidly melting snow to Holy Trinity where I took baptismal vows in William's name as his godmother. Tolly stood as his godfather.

Joan was worn out by her ordeal, and for the first weeks she seemed incapable of caring for the newborn. When I put the infant to her breast, she could not bear to have him suckle. I prayed for her recovery for the child's sake, but in the meantime I took over in her stead, feeding

William barley water with a little honey. Slowly both mother and babe seemed to strengthen.

Then in April William was seized by a fever. Night and day I held him, sang to him, bathed his burning body with wet linen cloths. It was useless. At the end of six days William's soul left his tiny body. I carried him again to the church, this time to see him buried beside his two brothers, and mourned as if it were my own child taken from me. My stepmother, benumbed by her loss, neither wept nor spoke, and for days she took so little to eat or drink that I feared we would lose her as well. I did the grieving for us both.

But life, however painful, does not cease for the living. My stepmother gradually returned to her daily chores. We did not speak again of her dead child—it was almost as if William had never existed. On the other side of Shottery Brook, Emma prepared for her wedding to Robin. My father arranged through John Shakespeare to buy a pony and a new cart as well, adding that sum to the amount of the loan. And John told us that Mary Shakespeare was pregnant again.

Once we had the cart and pony, Joan resumed her ale-brewing and I resumed making the deliveries in Stratford. John Shakespeare had been replaced as ale-taster by a butcher in High Street. I missed my stops at the Shakespeares' house for the sampling, but the stop at the butcher's was simple and quick. Catty often came with me, and she always asked that we proceed very slowly past the King's New School. "Mayhap we'll see our Tom," she said.

I understood that the one she hoped to see was not our Tom but Edward Stinchcomb. Catty clung stubbornly to the hope that fate would again throw the teacher into her path. Every Sunday, when she should have been at her prayers, Catty fastened her gaze upon Usher Stinchcomb as he took his place in the chancel to assist the vicar.

Though I could not help but recall the kisses I'd once enjoyed by the Clopton Bridge when I was sixteen, I tried to reason with her. "What are you thinking? Edward Stinchcomb is nine years older than you. Better to meet boys of your own age at sheepshearings and mayings and harvest festivals. Someday you'll chance upon the one who will make a proper husband for you when you're of the proper age."

She threw me a pitying look. "You're old enough," she said. "And it hasn't happened for you."

"Not yet, but it surely will," I said, though I had moments of doubt: *What if it doesn't?*

———

The mood at Hewlands was so despairing after the death of the infant William that I often sought refuge with Emma. One day in mid-May I found her stirring the contents of an iron cauldron over a small fire in the garth behind Fulke's cottage. The smell was worse than a reeking chamber pot, for Emma was dyeing a length of woolen cloth for the new petticoat she would wear to her wedding. Indigo required urine as a mordant, so that the wool would take the dye. Making sure I was upwind, I sat on a stump while Emma stirred the evil-smelling brew.

But if I had counted upon Emma to lift my spirits, I was disappointed; her mood that day was nearly as dark as mine. I wondered if something had gone wrong between her and Robin.

"You seem troubled," I ventured at last.

"Aye," she admitted. "I am. But you must give me your most solemn word that you will speak of it to no one."

I gave her my word and waited as tears rolled down Emma's plump cheeks and dripped into the cauldron. "Tell me," I said.

"Agnes, I've only just learned that Robin practices the old faith in secret. He has confessed to me that he's a Catholic."

This revelation took me by surprise. "'Tis a dangerous thing he does," I said.

She shook her head and pressed her lips together. "I know," she murmured. We lapsed into an unhappy silence as Emma's tears flowed unchecked and I pondered her situation. "How did you learn of this?" I asked.

"He confessed it to me, but I've had my suspicions for some time. Since boyhood Robin has spent much of his time with Vicar John Frith at the church in Temple Grafton. The vicar's real love is hawks and other birds of prey, and Robin often helps him tend to sick or injured birds. Robin says 'tis near miraculous how he cures them."

Emma gave one last brisk stirring to the dye pot. I helped her lift out the cloth, now colored a deep blue-violet. "Often, when Robin and Vicar John worked together with the birds, binding up their wounds and dosing them with herbs, the vicar would talk about the glories of the old faith. Robin wants to be married by Vicar John in Temple Grafton, but my father will permit no such thing. He claims the vicar is well-known to be unsound in the Protestant faith."

We carried the cloth to the brook to rinse it. When the water ran clear, we squeezed out the cloth, Emma twisting one way and I the other, and spread it in the shade of a hedge to dry. Emma tossed a few faded garments belonging to her mother into the dye pot to revive their color, and we sat down to wait while the dye took. Now and then Emma rose to check the depth of color in the cloth.

"What will you do?" I asked. I rubbed the third part of the ring Robin had given me at their handfasting, the part that would soon be united with the other two on Emma's finger—unless something went amiss.

"Do?" Emma looked at me as though I had asked a silly question. "Why, marry him, of course! Mayhap then I can change his mind."

CHAPTER TEN
Ned Stinchcomb

HE BANNS of matrimony were cried at Holy Trinity for three Sundays in June, and on a day of brilliant sunshine Emma and Robin walked together from Shottery to Stratford in a procession that included their families and ours and the Debdales with others gathered along the way to the church. Emma wore her indigo petticoat and a wreath in her hair that I had woven of pink and white roses. We were met at the church door by the vicar, William Smart, staunchly Protestant in his square cap and plain black gown.

I stood beside Emma as she and Robin exchanged their vows, the three narrow bands blessed and placed on Emma's left hand, and the marriage recorded in the parish register. Then the joyful couple led the way to the Bear, an inn near the Clopton Bridge, for their wedding feast. I walked behind them, keeping an uneasy eye out for Stephen Richardson, who was sure to show his ugly face at any moment; I had spied him among the wedding guests.

But it was Will Shakespeare with his winning smile who fell into step with me. "May it please you to allow me to escort you, Mistress Hathaway?" Will asked, tucking my hand into the crook of his elbow even before I could reply aye or nay. When we reached the Bear, I thanked him. "No need to devote yourself to me, Will. Go and enjoy yourself, I beg you."

But Will, now fourteen, did not listen to me, and I confess I was glad of it when the dancing began and Will insisted upon leading me through the lively steps of the trenchmore.

❧

Though the newlyweds stayed with Fulke and Martha Sandells during the haying and the barley harvest, I saw much less of Emma once she'd become a wife. She seldom came to work in the flax field, and I had to beg Catty's help. Then at summer's end Emma's eldest brother moved his pregnant wife and their four children into Fulke's cottage, and Emma and Robin decided to make their home at Robin's parents' croft near Temple Grafton. Now I would see her scarcely at all.

With a heavy heart I helped Emma pack, and when the day came for them to leave, I hung shamelessly on her neck and wept. "I can't bear to have you go, Emma!" I cried.

"Whisht," she murmured, wiping away tears of her own. "'Tis not much over an hour's walk, if you don't dawdle. You'll visit me, and I'll come here, and we'll talk and laugh and tell each other secrets, just as we always have!" But neither of us truly believed it would be that way, and we both wept all the harder.

After one last embrace Emma climbed up beside Robin in George Whatley's oxcart and drove away. I watched until the cart disappeared from sight, then went to sit alone by Shottery Brook.

I was now two-and-twenty; it had been six months since my exchange of angry words with Joan, who seldom missed a chance to make me feel unwelcome, though she was careful not to make her cutting remarks in my father's presence. For my part, I held my tongue and tried not to let her cause me to lose my temper again. I was still several years short of spinsterhood; except among the nobility who betrothed their daughters as early as possible, women of my class—a yeoman's daughter—often did not marry until they were five-and-twenty. Still, my stepmother wanted me gone, and I was eager to go—when *the right man* came along.

As I sat brooding on the qualities I wanted in a husband—"too much," Joan would have said—Joan Little appeared by the brook and shattered my solitude. "What are you doing here?" she demanded. "You're wanted at home. *Now.*"

"I'll come when I'm ready," I said. "Don't bother to wait for me." Had I been so sullen and spiteful at the age of twelve? Doubtless my stepmother would have said so.

Wit, I thought, returning to my list, *kindness. Honesty.* To those I added, *cheerfulness and a pleasing demeanor.* Eventually I stood up and prepared to go home. *Dances well.*

❧

Twice each week Catty and I made the rounds together, delivering ale to Joan's customers. But when we stopped to exchange full jugs for empty ones at the mercer's shop by the King's New School, Catty for once did not beg me to go slowly, or even to pause beneath the open window of the schoolroom on the upper floor. I glanced at her. "Shall we not stop here?" I asked.

"Nay," she said with a resigned sigh. "'Tis no use. Usher Stinchcomb doesn't even notice me when we pass in the street."

But the pony, a creature of habit, had already come to a halt. "Let me try something," I whispered, and I began to imitate the song of the nightingale.

"Listen," I heard the teacher say to his pupils. "Who can tell the name of that songbird?"

I repeated the trilling notes and heard Tom's laugh, quickly stifled. Tom had recognized the whistle and the whistler.

"Thomas Hathaway, perhaps *you* can tell us the name of the bird," the usher said sternly. I accommodated him by a third imitation.

"I believe 'tis a nightingale, sir."

Catty nudged me, and next I mimicked the song of a lark.

"And that?" the teacher asked.

"A lark. If we wait a moment longer, mayhap we shall hear a linnet as well."

I was about to oblige with the linnet's song, but Catty shook her head. "As I told you, 'tis no use," she said with a wan smile. "Let us be on our way."

I flicked the reins and we drove on. I glanced sidelong at my sister, wondering if she was truly over her yearning for Usher Stinchcomb.

A fortnight later on a warm September day I was at my market stall when the Guild Hall clock struck eleven. The pupils scattered, racing toward their half day of freedom. I had begun to gather my unsold wares when I noticed the teacher making his hesitant way through the market cross toward my stall.

"Good morrow, Mistress Hathaway," he greeted me soberly.

"Good morrow to you, Usher Stinchcomb," I replied, somewhat surprised that he remembered my name. "May I offer you a sample of honey, the sweetest in all Warwickshire?"

Edward Stinchcomb tasted the honey, gazing at me with mild blue eyes. "The birdsong—was it you, mistress?"

"Aye, it was indeed," I admitted. "But how did you know?"

"Young Thomas Hathaway confessed knowledge of it."

The conversation continued haltingly until he purchased a lump of beeswax. The wax, I assured him, would provide the best care for his lute.

"And how did you know that I own a lute?" he asked, smiling.

"Will Shakespeare once told me he wished to study with you."

"Ah, Will Shakespeare! And so he has, for some months now. The lad has natural ability. He composes songs, both words and melodies, of a very high order.

But"—Edward Stinchcomb shook his head regretfully—"he refuses to practice, or he would be even better."

Before we parted, the teacher decided to purchase a portion of honeycomb, but he had nothing in which to put it. I offered the loan of a small dish, which he promised to return on the next market day.

The following week he kept his word. "The honey, Usher Stinchcomb, was it to your liking?" I asked.

"Indeed it was, Mistress Hathaway. The sweetest I've ever tasted."

"The beeswax? You found it satisfactory for your lute?"

"The instrument has never sounded better, and I think it must be due to your fine polish."

From that time on I looked forward to more visits from my bashful customer, for the teacher was a man of intelligence and good appearance. Sometimes he simply waved and smiled shyly and passed on. Sometimes he wandered absentmindedly among the other stalls, before stopping by mine. Then we had pleasant, if rather formal, conversations about the habits of bees, or the flowers they visited and the varieties of honey that were produced.

Doubtless, I should have mentioned these conversations to Catty, but I did not—they scarcely seemed worth noting. She no longer suggested that we stop beneath the window of the schoolroom. And because

Catty didn't speak again of the teacher, I hoped she had recovered from her foolish passion.

One day Edward seemed to lose some of his shyness and asked if he might have the honor of calling upon me. I was surprised. I was also hesitant, thinking of Catty. But I wanted him to and despite my uncertainty, I agreed that he could. I would tell my sister and make it right with her.

❧

The day after Edward spoke to me, my sister and I were in the barn, grinding windfall apples into a mash to be put through the cider press. Catty was turning the crank as I fed the apples into the grinder, and I struggled to find the words to tell her that Edward Stinchcomb had asked to call upon me. No matter what words I would have chosen, I doubt she would have reacted differently. She stopped cranking the grinder and stared at me.

"How could you, Agnes?" she cried. "You set a trap for him, even though you know I love him! I've loved him forever, and no matter what happens, I'll still love him forever!" Catty buried her face in her apron and bolted from the barn.

I ran after her. "Catty, I beg you, hear me out," I said, once I'd caught up to her and tried without much success to calm her. "I set no trap. He came to me. I did not do this to you. You are only sixteen, I'm two-and-twenty and Ned three years older! Forgive me, dear Catty, but Ned has paid you no attention whatsoever for months, and I assumed you had forgotten him."

"You assumed wrongly!" she screamed. "Why didn't you refuse him? I hate you! And Ned is mine! Mine!"

Nothing I said made the slightest difference. For days Catty would not speak to me. This was an awkward situation, as we shared the same sleeping pallet. For weeks she sulked when Ned came to call on Sunday afternoons, though he always made it a point to speak kindly to her.

Our courtship proceeded at a measured pace through the weeks of autumn. Ned was a man of careful deliberation. Though he liked to walk hand in hand with me, often in companionable silence, by Yuletide he had not yet kissed me. I had begun to wonder if he ever would.

Then Twelfth Night came round again, celebrated this time at the home of Henry Field, the tanner, in Stratford-upon-Avon. Henry's son, Dick, was a great friend of Will Shakespeare. In the course of the merrymaking Dick ended up with Catty, and Ned was soon forgotten. My sister became her merry self again, and we were as close as before Ned became my suitor.

———

One winter evening as Ned and I sat together on the oaken settle near the hearth, I confided one of my unspoken desires: to learn to write. I asked Ned to teach me.

I'd learned to read—haltingly, it's true—when Tom did. And when Tom learned to write, I'd wished that I had that skill as well, though—like reading—I didn't view it as having practical value. My father could neither read nor write. When his signature was required on a bill of sale or other document, he made his mark, a large, sloping *X*. I suspected that Joan would find my desire another reason to ridicule me. But the more thought I gave to it, the more I wanted to learn. If I was one day to become a schoolmaster's wife, the skill might even have certain usefulness.

Ned responded to my timid suggestion with a fond but doubtful smile. At first he didn't believe I could read, until I took down the one book Tom owned and truly liked, *Aesop's Fables*. I read aloud the story of the fox and the grapes, slowly but with scarcely any mistakes. I enjoyed seeing Ned's surprise.

"Thomas taught me when he was learning," I explained. "But when he entered the King's New School, I no longer walked with him to his classes, and my lessons came to an end."

"Reading can be useful as well as pleasurable, 'tis true," Ned allowed. "But what use has a woman for writing?"

"I want to be able to write my name, not just sign with an *X*. Someday I may wish to write you a letter. Therefore I must learn to write proper words as well."

He considered this. "Then I shall teach you," he agreed.

On his next visit Ned brought me a gift of inkhorn, goose quill, and paper. He showed me how to mix the ink and sharpen the quill with a penknife, and the careful lessons began. *Agnes Hathaway,* he demonstrated, in what he called the italic hand.

"Your name," he said. "Now attempt to copy it."

I tried but made poor work of it.

"You must practice it letter by letter," he advised, "beginning with *A.* Just as you learned to read."

I continued to practice after Ned had gone, enjoying the looping *g* of Agnes and the middle *h* and final *y* of Hathaway. Within a fortnight I could write my name rather nicely. I hungered for more of the learning Ned could share with me.

But my stepmother grew impatient as the winter deepened and there was no sign of a betrothal. How long was this courtship going to last? I was beginning to wonder that myself. The truth was that I liked Ned and deeply admired him, but I felt little passion for him. I suspected that he felt the same way about me.

"Has he given no hints that he might soon propose marriage?" Joan asked.

"Nay," I said, "he has not."

"'Tis time," she said firmly. "Mayhap your father should speak to him."

But that wasn't necessary. Ned declared his intentions just before Lady Day in March and spoke to my father, who willingly gave the match his blessing. We would be handfasted a month later on St. George's Day. I was pleased. Ned would make me a good husband, I felt sure. I had not compromised. I cared for him. We would be happy. I hurried to tell Fulke and Martha Sandells the good news, and they promised to send word to Emma, asking her to be my witness. Catty seemed glad for me, and together we began to make plans for the ceremony.

There was a single dark cloud. Only days before my betrothal, the muffled bell at the Guild Hall tolled solemnly for Anne Shakespeare, Will's beloved seven-year-old sister, carried off by a fever. I was among the mourners who gathered in the churchyard under a sun that shone so brightly it seemed a mockery of the family's grief. The child, wrapped in a woolen winding-sheet, was lowered into the cold grave as the vicar intoned the words of the Psalmist: *The Lord is my shepherd; therefore can I lack nothing. He shall feed me in a green pasture, and lead me forth beside the waters of comfort....*

I saw Mary Shakespeare's wan and tearful face, John's as blank and expressionless as stone, the other children—Gilbert, Joan, and five-year-old Dick—with trembling lips and confused looks. But Will wore his anguish so openly that, when we met by the graveside, I felt impelled to touch his cheek and wipe away a tear.

Days later, before our families and a few close friends (but not the grieving Shakespeares), Ned and I promised to marry. I wore my best petticoat and bodice, Emma had given me a fine linen partlet trimmed in lace to wear round my neck, and Catty had woven a wreath of heartsease for my hair. My stepmother, satisfied that I had at last managed to find a match, roasted a young sheep as well as a fat goose.

We stood beneath the bower of roses that had been my mother's favorite spot. My father bound our wrists with a cord that I had woven of flax and wool. Ned placed one part of a silver ring upon my right hand, the second part on his own. Catty, serving as our witness, took the third part. We announced our intention to marry within the year and sealed it with a kiss. If I did not feel passionately in love, I believed—hoped!—I would in time. I was content that at last my future seemed assured.

❧

But no one can foresee the future. Within months, everything changed. In autumn another terrible illness swept through our shire. Now it was the sweating sickness that brought fear to every household. No one knew the cause, much less the cure—only that the disease struck the young and strong with particular vengeance, often leaving the old and weak untouched. Soon the mourning bell was tolling again and hearts were breaking.

When Ned was not in church on Sunday and didn't appear for his usual Sunday afternoon visit, I feared that he, too, had fallen ill. Tom offered to go with me to the usher's quarters by the Guild Hall. We found Ned alone and half mad with the ravages of the fever, his bed linens sweat-drenched and foul-smelling. I was not sure that he even recognized us. Tom ran to Alys Fletcher's to fetch food and drink and fresh linens, only to learn that Samuel, too, was ill, as well as one of their children, and Alys near collapse. No matter where we went to ask for help, we found suffering.

I sent Tom home and stayed by Ned's side to do what I could for him as he tossed and muttered feverishly. Hours later Tom returned with clean linens and mutton broth and the news that both my stepmother and Joan Little had fallen ill, and Meg, too. Catty needed me at home.

"But I can't leave Ned," I told Tom.

"They're sure to die without you, Agnes," Tom said, his eyes frantic with fear.

"So will he," I said quietly. "Tom, you must stay here with him. We can't leave him alone." I knelt by Ned's side and stroked his hand. "I'll be back as soon as I can," I whispered, though I doubt that he heard me. There was no time for weeping when people lay dying. I rose and prepared to leave.

Ned began to moan. "Tell me what to do," Tom pleaded.

"Pray," I said. I bent down and kissed Ned's burning brow, wondering if I'd see him again.

I hurried to Hewlands, where Catty and I dutifully tended Joan and Joan Little and Meg through the long, painful night. The next morning Tom stumbled home, exhausted and tearful. I knew what he would tell me even before he said it: Ned Stinchcomb was dead.

If I had been allowed to stay with him, mayhap I could have saved him. Instead it was my lot to save my stepmother and her daughters. It was a sin to believe that the wrong ones had been granted life while the good man was taken away. Nevertheless, that was how I felt.

Once the crisis passed for Joan and the girls, I walked alone to the churchyard and watched as Ned's cold body joined so many others I had known. And I listened with an aching heart as Vicar Smart intoned Psalm 130: *Out of the deep have I called unto thee, O Lord; Lord, hear my voice; O let thine ears consider well the voice of my complaint....*

I sorrowed for weeks after Ned's death. Not only had I lost a man who cared for me, but I had lost my future as well. Finally Joan, fully mended and more spiteful than ever, chided me impatiently, "Stop your whining and complaining and get on with life, Agnes—as I myself did when my husband and my child were taken by the plague, and then my newborn, and lastly my infant William. You're not the only one to suffer loss and pain. Mary Shakespeare buried a child last spring, yet now she's expecting another. Only God knows why things turn out as they do."

However much I resented the harshness of Joan's advice, I had no choice but to heed it. At winter's end I helped with the lambing and found that bringing new life into the world had a brightening effect on my own life. In April John and Mary Shakespeare presented their new babe, Edmund, for christening.

On May Day when Emma and Robin walked from Temple Grafton to visit her parents, Emma came looking for me. She'd hardly stepped across Shottery Brook before confiding eagerly that she was expecting a child in October. I was happy for her, and envious, too. Emma had found the life she wanted, while my future remained clouded and far out of reach. Ned's betrothal ring lay with my other mementos in the small wooden coffer on the shelf.

CHAPTER ELEVEN
•The Glover•

MY STEPMOTHER was convinced that the Shakespeares would not come to the sheepshearing festival in June. They were avoiding all public occasions because of John's financial problems, she said, repeating gossip she'd gathered from Alys.

"Even naming their newborn babe for Mary's wealthy brother-in-law, Edmund Lambert, hasn't helped John's situation," Joan said. "Lambert took the mortgage on Mary's property in Wilmcote, but he claims John owes him other debts. They've already lost a house and a piece of land. Every farthing John Shakespeare gets his hands on slips through his fingers like water. He dares not even attend church, lest the bailiff haul him off for indebtedness. Seems he'd rather pay the fine for not attending."

My father looked away as she rattled on. "John's been a good friend," my father said softly through clenched teeth. "He was generous to make me a loan for the barn when I needed it. I can't be overly critical of him."

"Best you watch he doesn't cheat you on the agreement for the wool," she said, tight-lipped.

My father slammed his hand on the table and walked away.

❧

Joan was only partly right—John and Mary did not attend the festival, though Will did. I was pleased to see him. Dick Field, Will's good friend who had shown great interest in Catty at Twelfth Night, had recently gone up to London to be apprenticed to a printer, and Catty was downcast. I had the notion that Will might be just the person to lift her spirits. Will was sixteen, a year younger than Catty, but he seemed older. When I saw him alone, I hurried over, intending to ask him if he would dance with my sister.

"Well met, Anne!" he greeted me. "Have you come to ask me for a dance?"

"Aye, but not with me. I come to beg a favor."

He clicked his heels and bowed with a flourish. "Your wish is my command."

"It's about Dick Field," I began. "And my sister Catty."

"So it's Dick you want to talk about. The lucky dog! How I should like to be in London! I miss Dick. There's no one to catch coneys with me, or to poach a deer once in a while."

"Poach a deer!" I cried, genuinely shocked. "Surely not from Sir Thomas Lucy's estate! You'll be caught, and whipped for certain, and mayhap sent to prison."

"Once in a *great* while, Anne! 'Tis a game of skill— to prove that one is canny enough to carry the doe past the gamekeeper's nose."

"But if you should be found out!" I said, remembering the bloody stripes on Kip Swallow's back.

"But I shall not," he said, smiling. "Now, are you going to ask me to dance?"

"With my sister Catty. She's missing our friend Dick Field. I thought you might cheer her."

"But first with you—unless you have no need of cheering?"

The dance, called a hay, was more elaborate than our usual country dances, but Will, always a graceful boy, led me easily through the interweaving steps. "I've been taking lessons," he confided.

"Whatever for?" I asked. "Has the queen asked you to dance at court?"

"Nay, but do you remember I once told you that I hope to become a player as well as a poet?"

"Aye, I remember." I missed a step and stumbled a bit but Will covered it well, and we continued on.

"A player must be able to behave as a gentleman does, and know all of the gentlemanly tricks—bowing, escorting a lady, and, most of all, dancing." The music stopped. "A player must know the court dances, be-cause—have you not noticed?—many plays involve dancing. So, when the last company came through Stratford, I asked one of the players to teach me some steps, and he obliged. But you're the first partner I've had with whom to practice."

Will filled our tankards with spiced ale, and while he described his dream of becoming an actor, began to wander toward Shottery Brook. Caught up in his de-scription of the life of a player, I drifted along with him.

"I must learn to fight with sword and dagger," he ex-plained, "or at least to look as though I really know how to fight with sword and dagger."

He spread his doublet on the grass near the water, and we sat down, side by side. He talked, and I listened. Will was always good company, and I was not displeased to find myself alone with him. Suddenly Will leaped to his feet and, seizing a long stick, began to demonstrate some graceful thrusts and parries.

"Sword-fighting is not as difficult as using daggers," he said. He broke his long stick in two and tossed half to me. "Come, Anne, stand up and let me show you."

I had no interest in learning to feign stabbing with a dagger on the stage, but Will's enthusiasm was infectious. "Now, with my back to the audience, I thrust the dagger toward you, like this, and it slips under your arm, and then you squeeze the bag of blood that you've concealed beneath your costume, and—"

Will lunged, and I moved my arm aside so that the make-believe dagger would pass under it. But I must have moved the wrong way, or Will miscalculated; in either case we collided, and I lost my balance and toppled over backward. Will stumbled and fell forward. We landed in a tangled heap on the grass, his face just inches above mine. We stared at each other. And then he kissed me.

I was the first to come to my senses. I pushed him away and scrambled to my feet, breathless. *What am I doing here with this boy?*

"Pray pardon, Anne!" Will cried, blushing. "I crave your forgiveness, I never intended—," he stammered.

"Never mind what you intended," I said crossly and clamped my arms across my chest. "I've had enough of your instruction in stage fighting."

Will recovered himself quickly. "That part is more difficult than dancing," he said, unperturbed. "But the most challenging of all is learning to play all those musical instruments!" He lowered his voice. "You know, do you not, that Ned Stinchcomb was teaching me to play upon the lute?" he asked, as though nothing out of the ordinary had just happened.

I nodded. "He told me that you had a particular talent for it," I said, my voice still unsteady. *How can he be so calm?*

"Now I'm struggling with the cittern. I've heard that bass viol is useful as well."

"You must learn all of this in order to become a player?"

"Aye, I must."

"I thought 'twould be enough to learn the words!"

"That's the easy part," he said. "Now come, Anne, and let me teach you the steps for a pavane."

"Another day," I said, eager now to be away from him and his unbounded enthusiasm. "High time I get back to help my stepmother. She surely wonders what has become of me. And you might look for Catty," I added. "Remember that you promised me you'd have a dance with her."

That night after the last guest had left and everyone at Hewlands had fallen wearily onto their pallets, I was nearly asleep when a voice hissed in my ear: "I saw you." It was Joan Little.

"What?" I murmured. "What do you want?"

"I saw you and Will," the wicked girl whispered. "I saw you lying on the ground together, kissing."

"You only *think* you saw such a thing," I mumbled, pulling the rough woolen blanket over my head. "And you'd be wrong."

"I know what I saw," she insisted. "Enough to tell the bawdy court."

Under the blanket I clenched my fists, and my body stiffened with anger. *A pox upon you, impertinent brat!* I thought.

When we dragged ourselves out the next morning to begin our chores, Joan Little followed me into the cow byre, miming a kiss. "Bawdy court! Bawdy court!" she taunted, and ran away laughing.

I wanted badly to slap her, to pinch her, to twist her ear until she howled, but this would have brought her mother's wrath down upon me. And so I did none of these things, deciding instead that the best course was to ignore her and hope that her threats were all bluster.

❧

Lowering skies unleashed downpours day after day, and we were hard-pressed to get the hay cut and into the barn, the barley reaped and threshed, the flax dried and ready for spinning. That year's hired harvesters had proved to be a sluggish lot. Catty, Tom, Joan Little, and I added our labors—even young Meg tried to help— but the heaviest load fell upon the shoulders of Tolly and my father.

There was no time to make the long walk to visit Emma on the far side of Temple Grafton, and I did not see my friend again until her infant daughter, Cicely, was christened at St. Andrew's, their small parish church. It was a crisp October morning, the sky strewn with lacy clouds. The old priest, Vicar John Frith, poured water on the infant's head and pronounced the words, a situation that must have troubled Emma's parents. We then walked the half mile to the Whatleys' cottage to present our gifts and drink our toasts.

Mistress Whatley, Robin's mother, hovered protectively over the cradle. Emma rested nearby on a settle, looking tired and drawn—mayhap her labor was hard,

I thought—and Robin strutted round like a cockerel, receiving congratulations.

"Come back as soon as you can, Agnes," Emma whispered when I bent to kiss her. "I do miss you so!" I thought I saw tears gathering in her bright eyes but put it down to weariness and excitement.

Nevertheless, feeling that something was amiss, I set off a few weeks later for Temple Grafton. The wind had a cold edge that cut like the blade of a knife, warning of a hard winter to come. I was glad to reach Emma's home, one snug room, a loft, and a larder built onto the rear of the elder Whatleys' cottage. Tiny Cicely was red-faced and howling, and Emma was trying frantically to soothe her.

"If she hears, she'll be over in a trice!" Emma complained, jiggling the infant against her shoulder.

"Who, Emma?" I asked.

"My mother-in-law. She gives me no peace, Agnes! Whenever she hears crying, she rushes in and snatches my babe away from me, and sometimes even takes her to her own rooms without so much as a by-your-leave. And she tells Robin I'm not a good mother, that my milk is too thin, that the babe will not thrive! Oh, Agnes," she sobbed, "I'm so miserable, I don't know what to do!"

And, indeed, I had not seen her so desolate since her visit to the bawdy court. "Have you some eggs and a little cream? I'll make us each a posset cup, and then we'll sit and have a good talk. Once you're calm, the babe will be calm as well."

I found what I needed and set to beating the eggs and cream over the flickering fire in a poor hearth, adding a grating or two of cinnamon and a good dash of ale. By the time I'd finished, Cicely had cried herself to sleep, and Emma and I sat quietly by her cradle, comforting ourselves with the hot posset. Out of habit I picked up a distaff from Emma's basket and began spinning while we talked.

"That's another thing," Emma said. "My mother-in-law complains that I don't do enough. She claims that she nursed her twins while she raked hay, threshed barley, and scutched flax, and that she was never without a spindle in her hand. She says I'm slothful!" Emma began weeping afresh.

"Nay, Emma," I said. "Not you."

But as if to prove Emma right, Mistress Whatley shortly sailed through the connecting door without so much as a knock or a call. A stout woman, she stood with feet apart and fists planted on her ample hips. "So, this is how you spend your time? Lolling about and indulging yourselves? It must be that girls in Shottery are spoiled to live an easy life!"

"Mistress Whatley!" I sang out cheerily. "Let me fix

you a posset cup so that you may take a well-deserved rest from your ceaseless labors while the babe slumbers!"

The woman eyed me suspiciously as she plumped down on the settle. I added a large dollop of ale to her posset cup, tipped in a bit more, and served it to her. For a while we sat peacefully. When Mistress Whatley appeared to nod off, I took advantage of the moment to whisper to Emma, "I must start for home. Will you walk with me a way?"

Emma quickly grabbed her shawl, and we tiptoed out the door while babe and grandmother drowsed by the fire.

"So you see how it is?" Emma asked.

"Aye, I do. But you have Robin and a lovely babe, and for those blessings you must be grateful. Mayhap you'll soon have a croft at a distance from the parents, and all will be well."

"Mayhap," Emma sighed. Then she stopped and peered round, making sure we were not overheard. "The mother is trouble enough, but there's more to tell. I've heard Robin talking with his father late at night about the old faith. The pope is sending priests from Rome to minister to England's secret Catholics. There's talk of sheltering one of them, Thomas Cottam, right here. His brother, John Cottam, is the new headmaster at the King's New School. Mayhap you know him."

This frightened me. "Have you spoken to Robin of the danger?" I asked.

"Nay, Agnes, I have not. I was eavesdropping, and I can't bring myself to mention what I heard."

"But you must! If the priest is found out, you will all be in risk of your lives. Did you not hear what happened to Robert Debdale, the Catholic priest? His father told my father that Robert was arrested when he tried to enter the country from France, and he was horribly tortured! Surely your father knows of it, too. For the sake of the infant, and your own sake, you must beg Robin not to get involved in this."

We walked a bit farther. "You're right, Agnes," said Emma. "I'll warn my husband, I promise you."

When we were within sight of the Alcester Road, Emma and I embraced. "You'll come again soon?" she asked.

I said I would, though I was not certain either of us could keep our promises.

❧

At Yuletide a company of players known as the Queen's Men came through Stratford, and as usual I made plans to attend. It turned out that Will Shakespeare had been invited to act in their play, costumed as a woman, and given two or three lines to speak. Women, of course, were forbidden to appear in plays, and female parts were taken by young men. Not until afterward, when he removed the feminine wig, did I recognize Will.

Due to a mild indisposition, I did not join the Twelfth Night revelries in Stratford a few days later. I was happy to avoid the unwanted attentions of Stephen Richardson, but I also missed seeing Will. I hadn't had an occasion to speak to him since the sheepshearing festival that ended with a clumsy accidental kiss many months earlier. Now I regretted not having the chance to ask him about his performance with the Queen's Men.

During the month of January I made a number of beeswax candles to sell at the market for Candlemas. It was the custom in many families to burn beeswax candles in honor of the Virgin Mary forty days after the birth of Jesus. My candles were of various sizes, so that even poorer folk might have at least one small beeswax candle to place in a window.

Market day had turned blustery with squalls of stinging snow, and though I was bundled in woolen stockings, petticoats, and a cloak, I could not ward off the chill. There was little business at the market, almost no demand for my candles, and I decided to leave early. I had finished packing when Will arrived at my stall, catching me by surprise. I was happy to see him, but

Will seemed at a loss for words, certainly unusual for him. Mayhap both of us were thinking of that kiss by Shottery Brook.

I tried to put him at ease, mentioning that I had seen him acting with the Queen's Men at Yuletide. Then I attempted a joke. "Doubtless you would have preferred a role in which to show your skill with sword or dagger!"

He brushed this aside. "I've brought news for you," he began. "And a gift as well. Which shall I deliver first?"

"A gift? For me?" I pretended to consider the question. "Well, then, the gift, if it please you."

"It *does* please me, Anne." He handed over a small parcel tied with hemp, which I opened to find a handsome pair of cheverel gloves. "As I promised you. I made them," Will explained. "They aren't my first pair, but they are my finest. Do try them."

I slipped them on. "Will," I said gently, smoothing the beautiful gloves over my fingers, "I can't accept these. They're worthy of Lady Lucy, or the wife of the earl of Warwick, not a yeoman's daughter!"

"They are worthy of *you*, Anne," he said. "And now that I have delivered my gift, 'tis time to deliver my news. I'm to leave on Monday for Lancashire, to be employed by a wealthy gentleman as tutor for his children. I shall be gone for some time. I wanted you to have this parting gift as a remembrance."

"Lancashire!" I exclaimed. "But that's more than halfway to Scotland!" My thoughts veered to Kit Swallow, who had fled northward to Yorkshire years ago and not been heard from since.

"Aye, I know that. But 'tis a good position, and I've even heard that the gentleman maintains a company of players at his mansion. My father arranged it through acquaintances. I don't have the license required to teach, but, living so far from London, the good squire doesn't seem to worry about formalities."

I removed the gloves, a finger at a time, and studied them closely. The stitching was fine and even. A dainty pattern had been worked in the backs. Examining the gloves gave me time to examine my feelings. I did not want Will to leave, but I was surprised by *how much* I did not want Will to leave.

"Will you write to me then?" I asked, placing the precious gloves in my pocket. "I can read, and I should like very much to hear of your life in Lancashire."

"Aye, that I shall," he said. "And will you write to me as well? Send me news of Stratford? Not the subject of Vicar Smart's Sunday homily but, rather, the naughty gossip—the names of those lately called before the bawdy court!"

"My writing is poor. Ned Stinchcomb was teaching

me. I learned to make the letters but have little sense of the words."

"It would cheer me just to know that it was from your hand," Will said, taking mine in both of his.

"Farewell, then," I said, nearly overcome by a rush of sadness. "And Godspeed."

"Farewell, dear Anne," Will replied. "Don't forget me, I beg you." He raised my trembling hand to his lips and kissed each finger, one by one.

CHAPTER TWELVE
•*Richard Hathaway*•

ILL WAS two months short of seventeen when he started on the long journey north to Lancashire. I thought of him often— Will Shakespeare was not a boy one forgot easily—and I sometimes thought of writing to him, as I had promised. But I was unsure of my ability with pen and paper, and what did I have to say to him?

My life continued much as it had before—Joan nagging, Joan Little taunting—but with one difference: I began to notice a change in my father.

Lambing season was always an especially busy time at Hewlands, the burden of the long hours with little sleep falling upon Father, Tolly, shepherd Thomas, and me. But that spring when the lambing was done, my father, always a strong and hearty man, failed to regain his usual vigor. Though he seldom complained, Catty and I whispered that he seemed not to be himself. Once, finding Tolly alone, I asked him if Father had mentioned feeling poorly.

"Nay," Tolly said, "he has not. But I, too, have observed that he seems weary."

By sheepshearing time it was plain that something was wrong, yet my father still pretended otherwise. Then one morning, as I hitched the pony to the cart to deliver Joan's ale, my father asked if he might ride into Stratford with me. Never in my memory had he made such a request, for it was not a long walk, scarcely two miles. Naturally I agreed, glad for his company.

"Where are you going, Father?" I asked as we rumbled toward the ale-taster's place in High Street.

"To the office of lawyer Wotton in Sheep Street, by Richardson's weaving shop."

I turned to look sharply at my father, who sat slumped in the cart. "May I ask for what purpose?"

"Drawing up my last will and testament," he replied, avoiding my eye. "I would be glad if you'd accompany me, Agnes. An inventory of goods is required," he added, "and I'll need your help remembering it all." He shifted his gaze to meet mine. "I believe that my time is coming, daughter, as it does for us all. 'Tis well to be prepared."

I swallowed hard and nodded, unwilling to betray publicly the pain such news gave me.

I left my father at lawyer Wotton's office and rushed through my rounds. When I arrived back at the lawyer's office, I found Father seated at a table with the scrivener, who had finished recording his wishes. I helped them prepare the list of my father's tools, clothing, furniture, and other possessions, the scrivener's quill racing over the parchment.

When my father was satisfied that all was in order, John Richardson was called from his weaving shop as witness when Father made his mark at the bottom of the document. He was so exhausted by the morning's effort that the weaver had to help him from the lawyer's office to the cart. Once home, I summoned Joan, and the two of us struggled to get my father to his bed in the upper chamber.

I ran out to the fields to find Tolly. "He's ill, Tolly," I said. "He had me take him to lawyer Wotton's office today, and he drew up his last will and testament. I feared we would not get home before he buckled. He has taken to his bed, and Stepmother is caring for him."

That evening at supper with Father absent from the

table, my stepmother exercised her authority. Soon it would be haying season; Father always hired the extra hands needed to cut the hay and later to bring in the barley. Joan directed Tolly to go at once to Fulke Sandells, tell him of Father's sudden decline, and ask his help in hiring laborers. Catty was to hurry to Wise Bessie in Stratford for herbal remedies. And Joan Little was sent to the wizened old woman near Drayton to purchase charms.

"As for you, Agnes," said Joan, "you are to stay at home to help tend him."

The tasks were accomplished. The harvesters appeared, accompanied by Fulke, who added his own labors to theirs. My father was dosed with nettle tonic, and a salve of wolfsbane mixed with almond oil was rubbed on his aching joints. A hagstone appeared over the bed where he lay, scissors open beneath it, a phial of salt by the doorpost. And I ran up and down from kitchen to bedchamber with broths and porridges and tempting bits of meat to try to strengthen him.

Nothing helped. I was sick with worry, and yet there was no opportunity to dwell on my fears, for much work remained to be done. So that we could attend to his needs more easily, we made up a bed for my father in the hall, a flock mattress laid atop a straw pallet with a sack of chaff upon which he could rest his head. On fine days he asked to be helped outside where he sat by the doorstep and looked out over the meadows and pastures that he had made so fruitful. But he was slowly wasting away.

My heart ached for Catty, who looked as though she might break in two, and for all the younger children, as well as Tolly, whose burdens had increased by manyfold. And I wished Emma still lived at the next farm, so that I could go to her and weep until there were no more tears.

❧

At the end of harvest season I received a visit from Emma, who'd brought little Cicely to her parents. How glad I was to see my dear friend! It was good to hear the chirp and chatter of a child's voice again in our gloomy household. I saw my father smile, however wanly, for the first time in weeks.

Emma tried to hide her shock: The once robust Richard Hathaway was now skin and bones and unable to walk on his own. "We must pray for him," Emma said, and I agreed that prayers were at least as useful as my stepmother's reliance on charms and strange mutterings.

Then it was my turn to be shocked, for as we knelt together by my father's side, I saw Emma slip from beneath her bodice a small wooden cross on a cord round her neck.

"What is that, Emma?" I whispered, once I'd said an amen to my prayer and she'd hidden the cross again under her clothing. "Is that not an object of the Catholic faith?"

"Aye," she replied, "'tis indeed. I've become one of them, Agnes. Robin wishes it so, but it is my own wish as well. Like him and many others, I believe that the Catholic Church is the one true church, and we must do all we can to keep the old faith alive. Promise you'll say nothing!"

My father's eyes opened briefly and gazed at each of us for a moment before they closed again. That night he fell into a deep stupor, where he lingered for a fortnight. Then he breathed his last and departed from this earthly life forever.

❧

We laid out my father's body on his proper bed in the upper chamber, where Joan and I washed it and prepared it for burial. Fulke Sandells and his wife were the first of our neighbors to come to pay their respects. Fulke, his eyes reddened, drew me aside while Martha murmured comfortingly to Joan.

"Your father asked me to be of particular help to you, Agnes. I remember well the day you were born, and I stood as your godfather when you were three days old.

I pledged then, and I pledged again to your father as he lay dying, that I am here to help you in any way I can." He leaned forward and pressed his dry lips upon my forehead.

I thanked Fulke, promising that henceforth I would regard him like a father. But even as I did so, I wondered if he had any notion that his own Emma had returned to the old faith with Robin, and that their path was strewn with danger and perhaps a terrible death if they were found out.

Shortly after my father's burial my stepmother produced the document that was my father's will and testament. Unable to read it herself, she did not trust me to read it truthfully or accurately. When I reminded her that her own son, Tom, had been the one to teach me to read, she agreed that he and I would read it aloud together.

"First I give and bequeath my soul into the hand of Almighty God and my body to the earth," it began. There followed a list of his bequests: Bartholomew as eldest son would inherit Hewlands, but he was charged with tending it so that it would support Joan and the children still living at home. Joan was entitled to one-third of all his goods, as was customary, and each minor child was granted a sum of money. My father had also specified certain token gifts to be made to his good friends Fulke Sandells and John Richardson and two or three others. Shepherd Thomas Whittington was to receive forty shillings in gratitude for his faithful service and the hope that he would remain in the employ of our family.

As for me, my father had dictated that I was to receive the equivalent of ten marks, which worked out to six pounds, thirteen shillings, four pence, a generous amount though not a fortune. But it was my dowry, to be paid to me on the day of my marriage, and not before.

❧

Less than a month after my father had been buried in the churchyard, Tolly startled us with his announcement. We were eating a quiet meal at the table, seated on joint stools, my father's empty chair reminding us painfully of his absence. Tolly cleared his throat. "I intend to marry Isabella within the month," he said. "The banns will be cried beginning Sunday next."

All heads at the table raised and all eyes turned to stare at Tolly. Joan spoke out at once. "How can you talk of a wedding when your father is scarcely cold in his grave?"

Tolly barely glanced at her. "I'm seven-and-twenty. I've kept Isabella waiting for two years since our hand-fasting while I worked with Father, as was my duty. I intend to wait no longer."

"Surely you're not leaving!" Catty exclaimed, her voice breaking.

"Aye, that I am—I've rented a small croft nearby. But I shall continue to till and mulch and sow the land under your direction, Stepmother. My father was concerned that a man's hand guide his family's welfare, and so I shall do his bidding, as I have in the past."

The meal continued in silence, each of us sunk deep in our own thoughts. Tolly was leaving, and I couldn't deny that it was time. *What of me?* I thought. *I'm five-and-twenty. Hasn't my time surely come as well?*

But I had no prospects. None at all.

❧

The autumn rains began. Another day of relentless downpour caused Shottery Brook to swell and the River Avon to rise, and few people came to the market. It was so late in the season that I had only a little honey left to sell. Scarcely anyone was interested in my lavender wands or beeswax candles. I thought I might not set up a stall again until spring, in order to save the toll due to the manager of the market. I was surprised, then, as I prepared to leave, to see Gilbert Shakespeare hurrying through the mud and rain toward my stall.

"Good morrow, Gilbert," I greeted him as he ducked under the shelter of the market roof. "What brings you out in such foul weather?" I asked.

"A letter from Will, mistress! Will sent it down from Lancashire by hackneyman enclosed with a letter to my family. Your name is written on it, and Will asked that I be certain to deliver it to you."

I marveled at this, for I had never in my life received a letter. Yet here it was, the precious paper folded several times, one end tucked into the other, and sealed with a wax wafer. I thanked Gilbert, gave him a bit of honey for his mother, and started for home, taking care to keep the letter under my cloak, safe from the pelting rain. I hurried straight to the barn, broke the wax seal, unfolded the paper, and carefully smoothed the single sheet, all the while wondering if I would be able to make out Will's handwriting.

Good friend Anne, he began, followed by an expression of hope that the letter found me in good health and high spirits. (At the time he had written, he would not have known of my father's death and of the changes that had inevitably followed.) Then he stated that his original employer had died in August, but not before recommending Will to a wealthy neighbor. Following a short stay with the second family, Will had moved again, this time to live with another wealthy family, Lord Strange, fourth earl of Derby. *And here I dwell most happily,* Will wrote, *teaching the younger children their letters and the older lads the basics of Latin. My happiness derives chiefly from the frequent chances to perform with Lord Strange's players, entertaining vast gatherings in the banqueting halls of Lathom House.*

Not only performing, Will went on to say, but also sometimes writing for Lord Strange's Men, and composing poetry when he found time. *I practice upon the lute and whatever other instruments come to hand, and I have written several songs that I shall gladly sing for you when next I see you, which time I hope will not be too far in the future.*

I spent a good part of an hour in the barn poring over Will's letter, often struggling, but finally assuring myself that I had indeed understood every word. I reread it aloud for the pleasure of imagining the sound of his voice. When I could wring no more from it, I folded the letter again and placed it in my wooden coffer, under the elegant cheverel gloves.

The banns for Tolly's wedding were cried, the wedding took place in mid-November before families and friends, and the couple went to live in a rented croft halfway between Shottery and Drayton. I was happy for my brother, though his absence from Hewlands was a trial for me. We were now mainly a family of women, and women who did not much care for one another.

Soon after Tolly's wedding, my stepmother came into the kitchen and spoke to me as I began to pluck a pair of old hens whose necks I'd just wrung. "Agnes, you are five-and-twenty, and you are just one more mouth that I can ill afford to feed," she declared. "Your father was much too indulgent. Had it been up to me, you would have been betrothed to Stephen Richardson regardless of your objections and wed to him by now. Ned Stinchcomb's death was a sad thing, but he has been in his grave for two years. Your days of doing as you please are at an end. You must marry, and the sooner the better. There is surely someone in this shire who would take you for a wife. I would advise you to get on with the business of finding him."

Though hardly unexpected, the harshness of Joan's announcement so stunned me that I was struck dumb. I gasped, struggling for breath like a fish thrown up on the shore, and stared at Joan. "Mayhap you already have someone in mind?" I managed to ask. "Someone not overly particular about what he gets?" I covered my hurt with contempt.

"In truth, I do," she said, ignoring my growing temper. "My nephew. His name is Henry Ingram, called Hob, and he works with my brother at the malthouse. You've doubtless met him when you've gone to Drayton to pick up the malted barley."

"I don't know any Henry Ingram," I muttered and continued furiously plucking the chickens. My stepmother was in effect throwing me out of the house, so eager to be rid of me that she would marry me off to the only man she could think of.

"You'll know him soon enough. My brother has invited us to Drayton for Yuletide," she continued undeterred. "He's thinking, no doubt, that I could use some cheering now that I'm a widow with five underage children and an aging spinster on my hands."

How I'd like to wring your neck as well, I thought. I flung the hens into an iron stewpot, pinfeathers and all, and fled from the kitchen.

❧

Christmas morning found Joan in her black widow's weeds with her five underage children and the *aging spinster* on their way to Drayton. We crossed fields thick with fresh snow that crumped beneath our feet. I was in a dark mood and hardly spoke—even to Catty, to whom I had repeated my wretched conversation with our stepmother. Joan's brother, Martin, and wife Bess greeted us cordially. There were others present, too, neighbors as well as relatives, and I did recognize the two men who had sometimes loaded the sacks of malted barley into my cart—one short, one shorter. I learned that the shorter one was Henry Ingram, called Hob, and from the way he grinned at me it was evident that he had already been told of Joan's plans for us.

Martin and Bess offered their guests a generous meal—shield of brawn from boar fattened on acorns and served with mustard sauce, and a currant pudding. They kept the wassail bowl filled with spiced ale until everyone was in a merry mood. Everyone but me.

I stole occasional glances at Hob, though to speak truthfully, there was not much to look at. He was of middling weight, with thinnish hair of a light color, smallish eyes the same, and a grin that displayed a missing tooth. He was not handsome, certainly, nor was he altogether ugly. He had little to say, and when he spoke, his words were simple, even dull. No wonder I had never paid him much attention when he'd loaded the sacks of malt into my cart. Now I was keenly aware of Hob's eyes upon me, though I pretended not to notice.

Later in the day when it was time to return to Hewlands, Hob asked if he might walk with me. Joan was watching me as an owl spies upon a mouse, and so I accepted. My sister Catty sent me sympathetic looks; Joan Little smirked.

I could think of nothing to say. Neither could Hob. We walked in awkward silence. I could scarcely wait to be rid of him. When we were within sight of our farm, he finally found his voice. "Mayhap we shall meet again on Twelfth Night," he said.

"Mayhap," I replied and watched with relief as Hob turned and headed back to Drayton.

"What ails you, Agnes?" my stepmother demanded when he was gone. "You were barely civil to him."

"I wasn't *un*civil," I argued.

"Listen to me, my girl," Joan said, her face close to mine. "This may be your last chance. Spoil it, and you'll likely end up in the almshouse."

The almshouse! I thought of the mean dwellings near the Guild Hall inhabited by indigent women, and my dislike for Joan reached new depths.

CHAPTER THIRTEEN
•*Hob Ingram*•

JOHN RICHARDSON invited us to a
Twelfth Night feast. I had no wish to go,
but my stepmother insisted: Hob was expected to be there. Then I learned that
Stephen Richardson was soon to wed a girl from Tiddington. This aroused my curiosity: Kit Swallow was
from Tiddington, and it was possible that Stephen's intended bride, whoever she was, knew Kit and might
even have some news of him. So, with Catty and Joan
Little, I set out for the Richardsons' house in Stratford.

Once I would have done everything possible to avoid
Stephen, but on this occasion I sought him out and
made a great show of congratulating him. At his side was
a comely young girl who gazed at him adoringly. *What*

can she possibly see in him? I wondered; whatever it was, I had surely missed it. The girl's name was Avis.

I tried to think of a way to separate Avis from her beloved long enough to ask a few questions, but this proved a difficult task. I would have to bide my time and watch for my opportunity. Then Hob Ingram spied me and laid claim to me.

I soon discovered that Hob did not like to dance. "Don't know how," he said as we stood off to the side, watching others take part in the trenchmore and the hay.

"Mayhap you could learn," I suggested. "'Tis not too difficult."

He shook his head. "Too clumsy, I am."

Nor did he appear to have much interest in music. When several young people moved to the weaving shop next door to sing catches, Hob begged off. My spirits, already low, sank farther. I remembered Twelfth Night at Samuel Fletcher's house, when I'd danced with Will Shakespeare in the hall and sung catches in the kitchen until I could dance and sing no more.

But Will was far away in Lancashire, and it seemed I would pass the evening thinking of those who were absent and of times gone by. Meanwhile, Hob had refilled his pot of ale numerous times and was growing decidedly tipsy. He'd had little enough to say throughout the evening, but as time passed, whatever he did say came out slurred. Finally, when he stumbled out to the privy, I hurried off in search of Avis.

I was in luck. Stephen, too, had stepped outside, and I found Avis alone. After I'd inquired politely of their wedding plans, I posed the question I had been yearning to ask all evening.

"I once knew a man from Tiddington," I said. "He worked for a time for my father, shearing sheep and harvesting hay and barley. Mayhap you're acquainted with him—Kit Swallow."

"Aye, Kit Swallow!" replied Avis, with a little giggle. "Promise you won't tell Stephen, but Kit and I were nearly handfasted once. And then he left for Yorkshire and broke my poor heart!"

"Ah, what naughty boys men can be!" I said, with a heartiness I did not feel. "Is there no hope then that he might return and mend your broken heart?"

"None," she replied, and I saw disappointment in her eyes—disappointment that I shared for myself. "His mother and sister received word that he wed his employer's daughter, once she discovered she was carrying his child."

I felt as though a favorite dish had just fallen from a shelf and smashed to pieces at my feet. There's no telling what turn this conversation might have taken, if Stephen and Hob had not returned from their business in the privy, and if I had not already learned more about Kit Swallow than I cared to know.

❧

Throughout the winter and into the spring, Hob made regular Sunday afternoon visits to our cottage. In bad weather we sat in near silence on the oaken settle by the fire, where I had once sat cozily with Ned Stinchcomb, learning to write. Hob had no such interests, nor did I expect it of him. Sometimes he spoke of the business of malting, and I listened with half an ear while I spun fleece or flax or knit woolen stockings for the younger children. When the weather warmed, we went for walks together, which I found more pleasant because Hob did at least share my fondness for birds.

At Eastertide Hob brought me a gift, a cage he had woven of willow branches in which a little nightingale was perched. It was so cleverly made that I found myself more kindly disposed toward him, and I squeezed his hand and rewarded him with a kiss.

"Agnes," he said, blushing a heated red, "does this mean we'll marry?"

What could I say? That I didn't love him? That I could barely tolerate him? I had allowed him to visit me for several months without turning him away. My stepmother had made it clear that I was to accept his offer, whenever he got round to making it, and to remove myself from her household as soon as possible. I felt neither joy nor sorrow. I felt nothing at all.

"Aye," I said, sensing that the door of my own cage had just snapped shut. "I consent to be your wife."

Hob dropped to his knees and began kissing both my hands while the nightingale looked on with a doleful eye.

Hob soon asked me to choose a date for our wedding. I hoped to postpone it as long as possible, but Joan disagreed. "It will be a year in September since your father died, and the money he left for your dowry is of use to no one," she pointed out. "Forgo the expense of a handfasting and marry at once."

The sooner you marry, the sooner you will be out of my house, she might have added. If only my father had left me the money outright, I might have moved away from the cottage and lived independently, at least for a while—even though I might have risked being accused as a witch and persecuted for it. But I couldn't claim my dowry until I married. I had no choice.

"We'll have the banns cried in September," I promised Hob. "And be wed in October."

Six months, I thought grimly; *six months until my fate is sealed forever. Six months until I marry a man I don't love and don't even much like.* It was just what I had vowed I would never do.

❧

The previous year's harvest had been a disappointing one, the result of a severe drought that parched many of the crops, and there had been no harvest festival. Now the Shottery farmers made plans for May Day to be celebrated on the village green, an ancient custom that all hoped would bring good rains and better yields that summer. Catty and I, with Meg and Jack tagging along, gathered primroses and cowslips for the maypole. When we reached the green, the village men had just hauled in a birch tree. Once they'd stripped it of its branches, my sisters and the other village girls decorated it with their flowers. Jack and I watched as the men raised the maypole and secured it in the center of the green.

A crowd had already begun to gather. Men set up tables, and women laid out their best puddings and sausages. Joan Little and Tom and their mother arrived, bringing jugs of ale. Musicians playing fiddles and bagpipes and pipe and tabors wandered through the crowd, as did a clumsy juggler who had trouble keeping the three balls in the air. Late in the morning some of the clever young girls and boys began to dance round the maypole and begged pennies for their performance.

Hob planned to arrive in the afternoon in time for the archery contest, and I'd promised to meet him at the butts on the far side of the green. Meanwhile, with time to spare, I bought a pennyworth of pigeon pie, for it was midday and I had eaten nothing since before sunrise. While I ate, I stopped to watch my brother Tom and a group of boys test their skill at knocking a penny off a peg by throwing their knives at it.

Then, hearing Joan Little's braying laughter, I went to watch her, and a boy I didn't know, engage in a game of tag called barley-break with two other couples. We still called her Joan Little to distinguish her from her mother, though *little* no longer described a wench who'd grown nearly as tall and certainly as broad as my father had once been. Her voice was loud and grating, her manner bold as brass, and she never hesitated to utter even the most stupid or outrageous opinion.

I didn't trust Joan Little, and I had good reason. Only days earlier I had overheard her and her mother talking in the alehouse while they filled the jugs. "She's a bad one," Joan Little said. "Burned down the barn, and if that wasn't mischief enough, she put a curse on Father, so as to gain an inheritance. Agnes is a witch," she insisted, "whether you want to believe it or not."

"Husht!" my stepmother said. "Don't speak so, or you will cause trouble for us all."

My stepmother had silenced her—not to defend me, of course, but only to protect herself.

I stepped into the alehouse, shaking with anger. The two started as though they had seen an apparition, and a full jug shattered at Joan Little's feet. "You will burn in hellfire for your evil words," I said evenly, and fixing them with a furious glare, I turned and left before they could answer me.

Now, keeping an eye out for Emma, I walked on across Shottery Green. I hadn't seen Emma for some months and hoped she might have come from Temple Grafton for May Day. Ever since she'd confessed her ties to the Catholic Church, I had worried about her. We'd all heard that Thomas Cottam, the Catholic priest, had been on his way from France to visit Stratford when he was betrayed by a spy and arrested in London. He was discovered to be carrying a letter from Robert Debdale to his father, our neighbor. And John Cottam, the headmaster at the King's New School, had quickly left when word reached Stratford of his brother's arrest. I remembered what Emma had told me: *There's talk of sheltering Thomas Cottam here.* If the authorities learned of the priest's connection to the Whatleys, it could bode ill for the family.

But suddenly, striding toward me and smiling broadly, came Will Shakespeare. I had no idea that Will had lately returned from Lancashire. To my eye he had changed completely. He had left Stratford more than a year before—still part boy, half grown, a beardless youth—and he had come back a man. *How handsome!* I thought. He laughed when he saw me staring at him openmouthed.

"How now, Anne!" he cried, opening his arms and sweeping me into his embrace. I was too startled to resist. "How I've missed you!" he said, his voice sweet in my ear. "Had I not found you here, I swear I would have gone to Hewlands to fetch you!"

I pulled away, aware that we were being observed: Joan Little stood off to the side, witnessing this scene through squinted eyes. "What brings you back to Stratford, Will?" I asked, when I had found my voice.

"My position came to an end, and I'd had enough of Lancashire and mayhap Lancashire had had enough of me. But come, let's walk, somewhere away from this crowd. I'll tell you all that's happened since I left, and I'll expect the same of you."

And, God help me, I went off with him, just as I had before, leaving the hateful Joan Little staring after us. For a moment I stared back. *Burn in hellfire,* I thought.

❧

Will led me toward Shottery Brook. We followed a path along the bank until we came to a thicket of young birches growing close by the stream. Inside the thicket it was like a chapel, cool and green, with a soft carpet of violets and wild thyme and a large, smooth rock, all well hidden from the path. Will sat down, stretching out his long legs, and drew me down beside him. Birds twittered above us, and the distant music of fiddles and bagpipes floated round us like a dream.

"Tell me of your adventures in the north, Will," I said. My heart was racing unaccountably, and I hoped he couldn't detect it.

"After you've told me first of yours," he replied. "You've been well, Anne? You are comelier than ever—lips like cherries, skin pale as a lily tinted with a primrose blush, eyes the very shade of bluebells—"

I felt the blood rise in my cheeks. "Aye, I've been quite well," I said. "But—mayhap you've heard?—my father died last September, a great sadness to us all. I intended to write to you of that and other matters, but—I beg your pardon—I did not."

Having only just returned from Lancashire, Will had not yet heard the news. "Ah, dear friend, what a grievous loss," he said, taking my hand. "I was truly fond of your father." For a moment we were silent. Then—without letting go my hand—he plied me with questions about my family. This would have been the opportunity for me to tell him about my stepmother's demands and my coming marriage to Hob Ingram. But I said nothing of that. Instead, I talked about Tolly's marriage and his struggle to manage Hewlands, now that the responsibility had shifted to him. Will listened with a sympathetic ear.

"Now," I coaxed. "'Tis your turn."

Will needed no coaxing. He launched into his narrative with enthusiasm. "My first employer, Alexander Hoghton, maintained a group of players, and I soon became a part of them. Being the youngest, I was best suited to play the female roles, which I much enjoyed."

He continued, "But Hoghton died soon after my arrival. He left his large collection of musical instruments and all manner of properties and play-clothes to a friend, Thomas Hesketh, who then invited me to join his household. Good fortune for me—and for them, too. His players found I had a quick memory. If a player forgot his lines, I improvised speeches to lead him back to his proper place. Anne, it was splendid!"

Pacing back and forth by the side of the stream, Will began to recite lines of dialogue. He had, I saw, a fine gift for mimicry as well as words. But the scene reminded me of an earlier time, two years past, when I had sat with Will by this same stream, and he had demonstrated his skill—or lack of it—with sword and dagger. That demonstration had ended with a kiss. I wondered if

Will, too, remembered it. I wondered if this, too, would end in a kiss. I feared—nay, hoped; nay, feared—that it would. But the moment passed, and I was disappointed.

"And I've been composing poetry. Did I tell you, Anne, that I've been working on the sonnet form?"

"You did write of this, and I thank you for your letter. But I know not what a sonnet is," I admitted. "Can you put it into plain words?"

"Indeed," said Will, commencing a long explanation. "A sonnet is a kind of poem, fourteen lines divided into three quatrains, followed by a couplet. Do you understand?"

Quatrains and a couplet? The look on my face surely betrayed my complete ignorance.

He stopped in the midst of his description and smiled down at me. "Never mind all that, dear Anne," he said. He dropped down beside me once more and began idly picking violets. "A sonnet is a love poem. You'll see."

All at once the air felt charged, as it does before a summer thunderstorm. I quickly changed the subject. "Do you intend to remain long in Stratford?" I asked.

"My father would like my help in the glove shop, but I haven't yet decided." He gazed at me. "Does it matter to you?"

"To me? Why should it matter to me?"

My thoughts bolted to Hob Ingram, who had no doubt arrived at the Shottery green and was surely looking for me, perhaps asking my sisters if they had seen me. Joan Little, who had observed me walking toward the brook with Will, would no doubt tell him, *She ran off with Will Shakespeare. They went that way.* And she would point out the path that led into the shadowy copse, a walk often taken by lovers. Hands on her broad hips, she would cock her head boldly. *Let's go look for them,* I imagined her saying. *I'll help you find her.*

Suddenly breathless, as though a heavy weight had settled upon my chest, I scrambled to my feet and glanced anxiously in the direction of the green. "I must go back," I said. "My sisters will wonder what has become of me."

"Wait!" Will leaped up, holding out a nosegay of violets. "These are for you, Anne."

I accepted the posy, my feelings a roiling sea of confusion, and hurried toward the music and the laughter.

CHAPTER FOURTEEN
•*May Day*•

ARMERS AND villagers had crowded Shottery Green for the May Day festival. I stopped to catch my breath and then, with the violets tucked in my bosom, started across the green toward the archery butts. When I passed Robin Whatley and Fulke Sandells playing at bowls, I knew Emma must be nearby. I found her at one of the tables, engaged in a game of primero. Emma saw me and threw down her cards. She hurried after me, six-month-old Cicely balanced on her hip.

"I've looked everywhere for you, Agnes," she said, offering me the babe to kiss. "No one seemed to know where you'd got to. Catty told me that you're planning to wed—she even pointed out your sweetheart to me—

but then Joan Little said you'd gone off into the bushes with Will Shakespeare! Which story is true? I thought Will was in Lancashire. So who is this sweetheart, and when was your handfasting? I would have expected an invitation, at the least. We have much to talk about, I'll wager!"

"Will has come back from Lancashire, that much is true," I said, "and I've agreed to marry Hob Ingram, so that is true as well. We've had no formal betrothal, but you may count on being a part of the wedding."

Emma threw her free arm round me. "I'faith, Agnes," she cried joyfully, "many times have I prayed for you to find a loving husband! You must tell me all about him! When is the wedding?"

"In little more than five months." *Five months,* I thought, *only five months left.* "Let me get us two pots of ale, and you shall hear all of it."

This done, we moved away from the green and settled ourselves in a sheltered spot near the smithy. Cicely, who had been whimpering, burst into insistent wails, and Emma put the babe to her breast. "Now," said Emma, "tell me about your sweetheart and your future plans. Leave out nothing in the telling!"

"There is little to tell. My stepmother gave notice that she wanted me out of her household and demanded that I marry as soon as possible. She proposed her nephew, Henry Ingram—called Hob—as a suitable hus-band. He was agreeable. He asked me to be his wife, and I've said that I will, come October. So there, you have it all." I sighed and wiped my eyes.

Emma looked at me sharply. "You don't love him—I can hear it in your voice, Agnes. You don't sound like a woman in love. Nor do you look like one."

"I suppose I like him well enough. He's honest and steady." But I couldn't continue the pretense. "Nay, Emma," I burst into tears, burying my face in my hands, "you're right—I don't love him. He has neither wit nor talent for conversation or dancing or anything much. I dread becoming his wife!"

Emma shook her head sadly. "Oh, Agnes, I do pity you! Love is such a glorious thing. I wish for you to have what Robin and I have."

"And a mother-in-law like yours in the bargain?" I asked, recalling Mistress Whatley's overbearing behavior during my visit.

Emma looked away. "Marriage is not always heaven on earth, 'tis true," she admitted. "But a babe makes up for whatever is missing."

I regretted my harshness and said so. "I'm envious, that's all."

Emma hummed softly to Cicely, who was suckling contentedly. I knew that I should go in search of Hob, but I was in no hurry either to find him or to leave this peaceful scene. And I still had questions for Emma. I wanted to ask about her Catholic beliefs, and if she and Robin were taking care to keep their outlawed faith a secret. But instead I said, "I *have* seen Will Shakespeare. He's here today."

"'Tis true, then!" she said. "Have you been with him? Ah, you have, I can tell by your look! Like a cat lapping up cream! Tell me more, Agnes! Did you go off into the bushes with him, as Joan Little claimed?"

"I've spoken with him just now, but it was not at all as that shameless Joan Little would have you believe! I was surprised to see him here. He told me of his adventures in Lancashire, in the households of several wealthy gentlemen. He went north as a tutor for Alexander Hoghton's children but ended, it seems, as a player with Lord Strange's Men."

Emma bent closer. "Staunch Catholics, both of them," she confided. "Lancashire is a hotbed of the old faith. If that's the way Will is leaning, he should have stayed in the north. I've heard that his father holds those beliefs, though you'd never guess it. John Shakespeare acts the Protestant but in his heart he's Catholic."

"How do you know this?" I asked. This news made me very uneasy.

"We all know it—those of us who share the old

faith." Cicely had fallen asleep at her mother's breast, and Emma laid her sleeping daughter on the grass between us. "Now tell all, Agnes. I suspect there's more to the story. Those violets in your bosom—did he pick them for you?"

"Aye, he did, but there's nothing more to tell," I insisted, though that was not quite true. *I wanted him to kiss me again. But he didn't.* I got up and brushed off my petticoats. "Now I must look for Hob. He's sure to be wondering what's become of his sweetheart." I nearly choked on the word.

Emma picked up her babe. "I'll come with you," she said.

❧

We found Hob at the archery butts. "Well met, Agnes," he greeted me. "Lost, were you?"

"Nay, Hob," I said, "not lost. I've been with my friend here, Emma Whatley and her babe, sitting in the shade over by the smithy." Hob and Emma acknowledged each other; he scarcely glanced at her, but she looked him over coolly.

"Not here to see me best all challengers?" he asked with a certain arrogance. Though short, Hob was very strong and skilled with the longbow. He boasted that he had easily defeated several young men eager to prove their ability.

"You haven't yet bested me," said a familiar voice. Will Shakespeare stepped forward. Emma and I exchanged glances.

"Is that a challenge?" Hob asked. He eyed Will, a stranger to him.

"'Tis, if you wish it so," replied Will. "Mistress Hathaway might enjoy the contest."

Hob threw me a questioning look. "You are acquainted with him?" he asked.

"Aye, I am," I said. "His name is William Shakespeare of Stratford."

Will picked up a bow, drew back the bowstring to test it, and then tried another. Hob and most of the other competitors had brought their own bows, but Will seemed satisfied to use one that had been left for chance passersby.

The contest began. The two archers were well matched, and soon a small crowd had gathered to watch. Will proved to be a fine bowman, shooting with a careless ease. Hob worked harder, the tension showing in his clenched jaw.

"'Tis for you they're doing this," Emma whispered. I clutched her arm.

As I watched, I found myself wishing that Will would prove the better bowman. I didn't understand my feelings. In five months' time I would be Hob Ingram's wife; why, then, did my heart leap whenever Will Shakespeare's arrow found its mark? I dared not let either man know where my feelings lay.

The match was close, but in the end Hob won by just two points, and though I was disappointed, I was also relieved. I was beginning to see that Hob Ingram had an angry side, revealed when things did not go his way. Will accepted his defeat gracefully, but Hob was not a gracious winner. He gloated and swaggered over to pull me out of the crowd of onlookers.

"Have you a reward for me?" Hob demanded. Reluctantly I bestowed a kiss on his cheek.

He wasn't satisfied. "You call that a kiss?" he growled, and he seized me by both arms. The nosegay of violets in my bodice fell to the ground. I hoped he wouldn't notice, but he did. "Hello, what's this? A lover's gift?"

My mouth opened and closed again as I searched for a proper reply. Emma stepped forward. "Nay, a friend's," she said with a smile, picking up the nosegay and tucking it back in my bosom.

Bless you, Emma, I thought.

The awkward moment passed. Will shook Hob's hand. "Do I understand that you and Mistress Hathaway are to marry?" he asked. "In that case, I congratulate you. You are both fortunate—you for having such a lovely mistress as your soon-to-be wife, and she for having such a splendid bowman as her soon-to-be husband."

I managed an uneasy and, doubtless, unconvincing smile, but I could not meet Will's eyes, or Hob's, or Emma's. I had not told any of them the truth of my feelings. My only wish then was that the day come to its end, and quickly. Will bowed and walked away.

After May Day Tolly and I planted the flax field, and the green shoots soon began emerging from the brown earth. My bees were swarming. The calves had to be separated from their mothers and put out in their own pasture. Catty delivered Joan's ale, and I sometimes went with her. Mostly, I looked forward to Thursdays, market day, glad of the chance to get away.

I had been unable to banish Will Shakespeare from my thoughts. On Sunday mornings at worship service, when he sat with his family and I sat with mine, no words or glances passed between us. But if we happened to find ourselves leaving the church at the same time, we exchanged guarded smiles and slight nods, as was proper between a young man and a woman betrothed to someone else.

Thursdays were different. Will was at the market, selling his father's gloves and leather goods, and he always came by my stall to pass the time of day. I looked forward to his arrival, and while I waited I thought of subjects we might discuss: I asked about his poetry, inquired when the next company of players might visit Stratford, spoke to him about music. Only with Will Shakespeare did I have such conversations.

But I was not the only woman eager to speak with Will. Since he'd come back from Lancashire, now a tall and handsome young man, girls flocked to him. I heard one name first, then another, mentioned in connection with his. None was serious, of course—at eighteen he was too young to marry, but not too young to flirt, or even to fall in love. Often I saw him strolling through Stratford with a comely young girl displaying her winsome smiles, her fluttering lashes, her coquettish laughter. When I saw him talking animatedly, leaning close, sometimes touching her shoulder, I had to look away.

❦

Late in May Will came to Hewlands to arrange purchase of the skins of Catty's young kids, and as luck had it, Catty was not at home. I was in the garden, weeding among the tender young parsnips and turnips, cabbages and fennel. When I heard Will's voice, I threw aside my hoe and hurried to greet him, regretting there was no time to wash my face or put on a clean apron.

I resolved to speak to him formally, as one speaks to a tradesman come to purchase skins, nothing more. "Good morrow, Will," I said coolly, but when he smiled at me, my resolve vanished like dew in the morning sun. We stood foolishly grinning at each other until I looked away. "You've come for cheverel?"

"Aye, e'en so. The new schoolmaster, Alexander Aspinall, has begun courting lawyer Wotton's daughter, Cordelia," Will explained. "He has ordered a pair of fine gloves as a gift for her."

"It will be my pleasure to help you," I said, sounding businesslike.

For the next hour we examined each kid in search of perfection, finally settling on two. With a promise to return in a fortnight to pick up the skins, Will went on his way and I picked up my hoe again, hoping that my stepmother and the ever-watchful Joan Little had taken note of what little importance Will Shakespeare was to me.

On the day Will was to come for the skins, I took pains to look presentable without attracting anyone's attention. But Will's brother Gilbert appeared in his stead, and my disappointment was no doubt evident to everyone—especially Joan Little, whose sneer seemed everlasting.

A few weeks later after sheepshearing, Will arrived once more at Hewlands, this time with his father. Since this was man's business, I had no excuse to be present and stayed busy in the kitchen. Tolly told me later that the price of wool had fallen sharply since the year before, and he was so disappointed in John's offer for the fleece that he had let the Shakespeares leave without inviting them to stay for the dinner I had taken pains to prepare.

❧

Hob continued to visit me on Sunday afternoons, and we began to discuss practical matters, such as where we would live once we were married. Joan reminded me that I must begin laying up a supply of bed linens, cooking pots, and other household necessities. I knew she was right, but I could scarcely bring myself to think about the future that loomed ahead of me like an advancing thundercloud.

Hob had once been so shy that he could scarcely bring himself to take my hand as we walked together, but in the weeks since I had agreed to marry him, he'd become amorous. He claimed I owed him my kisses, anytime, anywhere. Soon kisses were no longer enough.

"Come lie with me, Agnes," he begged as we walked one afternoon along the field path from Drayton.

I rebuffed him. "Not till we are wed," I told him.

"'Tis wrong for you to take my maidenhead before I am your wife."

"How do I know you're a virgin?" he demanded.

"Because I have told you that I am, and you must believe me," I said. His rudeness in questioning my virtue was insulting, and we ended up in an argument. He called me obstinate and shrewish. And I wondered that he would consider such insults the best way to persuade me to yield my virtue.

But my refusal—which he interpreted not as virtue but as stubbornness—only angered him. And his insistence angered *me*. In the end he begged my pardon, and I forgave him reluctantly.

Not a week later, the evening was still bright as we returned from the Midsummer Festival in Stratford. Hob had drunk great quantities of ale. His footsteps were unsteady, and I held his arm to keep him from falling.

"Stop here, sweetheart," he ordered drunkenly. When I did, he grabbed me roughly and began to cover my face with his slavering kisses.

I pushed him away. "'Tis neither time nor place for this, Hob. 'Tis unseemly."

He stumbled backward. "You refuse to kiss me?" he said and lunged at me again.

"Hob, I beg of you," I said, trying to free myself. "You're hurting me!"

He let me go, and we continued on toward Hew-lands, Hob staggering and cursing loudly. I tried to hush him, ashamed of the spectacle he presented. Passersby stared; some laughed; some frowned in disapproval. I urged him to hurry. When we entered a stand of alders on the far side of Shottery Brook, he fell upon me, knocking me to the ground, lifted my petticoats, and tried to force himself upon me.

Though he was much stronger than I, he was drunk and I was not. I clawed at him until I managed to get away. I heard him shouting "Harlot! Drab! Strumpet!" and other foul names, and I ran as fast as I could, slipping and sliding across the stepping-stones of the brook to the safety of my home.

Breathless and sobbing, I climbed the narrow stairs to my stepmother's bedchamber and awakened her. "Do as you wish, but I will not marry Hob Ingram!" I cried. "Never, never, never! Better the almshouse than a mansion with such a lout!"

I ran back down to the hall and paced, too upset and angry to sleep or even to lie down. Catty and Joan Little, who had returned earlier from the festival, sat up on their pallets.

"What's wrong?" Catty asked. "What happened?"

"Hob," I said, my voice trembling. "He— He tried

to—" I couldn't finish. "Look, my bodice is torn. My petticoat, too. And I lost a shoe in the brook."

My stepmother had descended the stairs and stood glaring at me. "I don't believe you," she said. "Doubtless you led him on with your wanton behavior, and now you try to shift the blame to him."

I stared at Joan, openmouthed and incredulous, wondering if I could have heard her rightly. "You believe him?" I asked. "And not me, whom you've raised as a daughter?"

"You are not of my blood," she said. "Not now, not ever." She turned and climbed back upstairs.

I had no right to be hurt—I had always known she despised me, but I felt deeply wounded. I would not, however, let her see how much. Catty rose and put her arms round me.

Joan Little stayed where she was. "Had it been Will Shakespeare in Hob's place," she said with her spiteful grin, "mayhap you would not be weeping so."

Catty gasped, "Hold your tongue, wicked girl!"

Quick as a fox, I reached down and seized a fistful of Joan Little's hair and hauled her to her feet. Though she was taller and stronger, I held the advantage of surprise and well-stoked anger.

"Mark me well, ill-tempered shrew," I hissed, "I have

had quite enough of your slanders. You've made me out to be a slattern, knowing that your loose tongue could have me brought before the bawdy court. You've called me a witch and accused me of causing our father's death to gain an inheritance, knowing full well how such accusations can end." I tightened my hold on her hank of hair and whispered menacingly, "Then let me say this, Joan Little: One more word from your deceitful lips, and you shall learn to your deepest sorrow what powers I *do* possess."

With that threat, I flung the astonished wench back on her pallet and stalked away, leaving her frightened and whimpering.

At first light I opened the cage of the nightingale Hob had given me and watched the bird fly away, wishing that I could escape as well.

❦

In the days following my declaration that I would not marry her nephew, my stepmother scarcely spoke to me. Her grim silences were interrupted only by occasional cruel words. Joan Little kept her distance.

"What will you do to her, Agnes?" Catty asked me.

I shrugged. "Nothing—I have no powers, but Joan Little doesn't know that. I just wanted to frighten her into silence."

"Well, you surely succeeded!"

"If only I could frighten Hob Ingram as well," I said.

Finally I turned to Tolly, who listened sympathetically as I described what had happened on Midsummer's Night. I begged him to carry a message to Hob.

"You'll be well rid of him," Tolly replied. "I never liked the man. Doubtless, you can do better than the likes of him. What would you have me tell him?"

"That I will not marry him."

Tolly did as I asked, returning with the word that Hob had muttered many blasphemous oaths but had at last accepted my decision.

"I didn't leave him a choice," Tolly said.

I was relieved to be done with Hob, but there remained Joan's demand that I leave her household. Mayhap, I thought, marriage was not the only way out. I cast about for another solution. Tolly might ask me to come to live with him and Isabella, though I knew a third person would be an unwelcome intrusion in their small cottage. Mayhap I could find a position as a servant with a gentleman's family. If my situation became truly desperate, I would ask Fulke Sandells to take me in for a time.

I prayed nightly that something would happen to deliver me from this dreary present to a brighter future.

CHAPTER FIFTEEN
•*Summer Love*•

S THOUGH mocking my bleak state, summer unfolded in a succession of warm days with skies as blue as my flax field. A golden sun coaxed sweet musk roses and eglantine into bloom, as well as lacy cow parsley and wild marjoram. It was the most beautiful summer in my memory, and yet the mood at Hewlands darkened. Mealtimes were unpleasant. Tempers grew short.

Tolly predicted that the hay crop would be bountiful this year, with just the right balance of rain and sunshine. Days before the haying was to begin in July, he came by to tell us how many men we could expect to feed.

"A half dozen," he said. "Four of them have worked

here in past years, two are new this season, one of them something of a surprise: Will Shakespeare."

Will Shakespeare coming here to work? I struggled to conceal the rush of feelings, while my stepmother scoffed, "Will Shakespeare! Our poet and playactor, cutting hay?" She let out a bark of harsh laughter. "Mayhap he'll seize a pen and scribble a few verses, or climb upon a stile and spout a few lines while others wield the scythes and rakes!"

"What do you know of his writing or his acting?" I demanded, though I knew it would be better to say nothing at all.

"Why, Agnes," Joan said, "'tis the talk of the town!"

❧

I scarcely slept the night before the haying began. *What folly,* I told myself severely, as I turned restlessly upon my pallet and tried to calm my racing heart. *You have known him since he was christened—since he wore napkins! He is much too young for you to be entertaining such yearnings.* But my heart took no note of what I told it and pounded all the harder.

The men arrived before sunrise, Will among them. Throughout the morning hours they worked steadily, stopping only for the bread and ale that my sisters took to them. I longed to be in the hayfield, but first I had to hoe the garden. I rushed through that chore and hurried out to the field.

Watching the rhythmic swing of the scythe in Will's hands, I was giddy with a heady mixture of irresistible attraction and grave misgiving. *He is only eighteen, with no real employment but what his father gives him,* I reminded myself sternly, *and you are nearly six-and-twenty and in need of a reliable husband.*

Late in the morning of the first day I made sure I was the one to carry the meal of ale and bread, cheese and meat pies to the men. Will accepted his ration with thanks. "Come sit by me, Anne." Ignoring the severe sermons I had preached to myself, I did so.

"Why are you here?" I asked. "You're neither laborer nor yeoman's son."

Will smiled. *Oh, that smile!* "Because the days are too fair to be spent at a glover's bench," he said. "And to see you, of course," he added, but in such a light tone that I doubted he was serious.

When he'd finished eating and drinking and the other men had stretched out under the trees with their hats tilted over their eyes, Will drew a stringed instrument from his knapsack. "I've brought my cittern," he said. "'Twas given me by my Lancashire employer.

Shall I play a song I wrote soon after I came home to Stratford?"

"Aye, if it please you."

Will corrected the tuning, strummed a few chords, and began to sing in a sweet tenor voice:

> It was a lover and his lass,
> With a hey, and a ho, and a hey-nonny-no,
> That o'er the green cornfields did pass,
> In spring time, in spring time,
> The only pretty ring time:
> When birds do sing, hey ding-a-ding, ding;
> Sweet lovers love the spring.

The men propped themselves on their elbows, the better to listen. But I felt that Will was singing only for me.

> Between the acres of the rye,
> With a hey, and a ho, and a hey-nonny-no,
> These pretty country folks would lie,
> In spring time, in spring time,
> The only pretty ring time:
> When birds do sing, hey ding-a-ding, ding;
> Sweet lovers love the spring.

Will let the last notes die away. The men listening from the shade of the hawthorns applauded loudly, and one of them let out a piercing whistle. "Do you like it, Anne?" Will asked.

"Aye, aye, I do," I said, too flustered to say more.

"I'm working on another verse or two," he said. "'How that a life was like a flower,' or some such." He reached over and tucked a stray lock of my hair under my kerchief, adding, "How Mistress Anne is like a flower." He replaced the cittern in the knapsack. "Time to go back to haying," he said. He rose and helped me to my feet. The men under the hawthorns stretched, groaned, and got up slowly.

Not until sunset did the laborers lay down their scythes. After we'd given them supper, those who lived in nearby villages made their way home, while others who lived at a distance prepared to sleep in the barn or outside under the stars.

Better that he leave, I told myself as Will set off for Stratford. *But what if he stayed?* I wondered. *What would you do then, foolish woman?*

❧

And so it went for four days. When the men stopped for their midday meal and rest, they called for Will to play his cittern. He knew many familiar songs—"Tomorrow the Fox Will Come to Town" and "Of All the Birds That Ever I See"—and soon had the men singing along. But his last song of the afternoon was always the one that began, *It was a lover and his lass.*

At the end of the fourth day the hay stood in golden sheaves, and the men collected their pay and prepared to move on to the hayfield of a neighboring farmer. Will left with the others. His leave-taking was brief, a wave of the hand and a simple "Fare thee well, I must away!"

"Will these same men return for the barley harvest?" I asked Tolly with as much indifference as I could feign.

"All but Will Shakespeare," Tolly replied.

"Nay? Not Will?"

"Says he's needed in the glover's shop."

I turned away, more determined than ever to banish all thoughts of Will from my mind. But again, I failed utterly.

❧

A week before the barley harvest, Tolly sent me to Stratford to buy the gloves for the harvesters. Dressed in a clean partlet and apron, fingernails pared, mint leaves chewed to sweeten my breath, I hurried to John Shakespeare's glove shop. There I found neither Will nor John but Gilbert, Will's younger brother.

I saw a pile of the three-fingered mitts. I was tempted to make excuses, not find what I was looking for, and promise to come back another time. But Gilbert was eager to make the sale, and reluctantly I bought what I needed. "Give my regards to Will," I said as I counted out payment.

"You can give them yourself," Gilbert replied. "Will's in the workshop behind the barn, finishing a pair of gloves ordered by the new schoolmaster. He'd be pleased enough to have a visitor." He jabbed his thumb toward the back of the property.

What has Will told him? I wondered as I crossed the garden, though Gilbert's face had revealed nothing.

I stepped through the low doorway into the workshop, a small, rather dark space with only a door and a single window to admit light and air. The pale white gloves were laid out on a worktable cluttered with stakes, shears, and paring knives. There was no sign of the glover.

"Will?" I said and waited. When I got no answer, I called more loudly. "Will?"

"Anne?" came the reply from somewhere above me. Long legs appeared on the crude ladder leading up to a small loft at one end of the workshop. "I have an aerie up there, a little nest," he explained. "That's where I go to write. The house is much too noisy for such work! Listen to this—I've written it for the schoolmaster to present with the gloves to Mistress Wotton:

The gift is small,
The will is all.
Alexander Aspinall"

"Very clever," I said with a laugh. "And you've slyly inserted your own name into it as well: '*Will* is all.'"

"You noticed! I wonder if Mistress Wotton and Master Aspinall will prove themselves as clever as you, dear Anne." He coughed and looked away. "May I ask if Henry Ingram intends to present you with such a gift? It would be my honor to make another pair for your wedding."

I shook my head. "We've broken off," I said.

Our eyes met, and for an awkward moment we gazed at each other. Will took one long step toward me. I hesitated, but only for a moment. Then with a deep breath I took one long step toward Will and closed my eyes.

A moment later we heard Gilbert shout from the house, "Mistress Hathaway! Mistress Hathaway! You've forgotten the gloves!"

❧

That was the first of many kisses, and I welcomed each one of them. From that moment on I wanted to spend every minute, every hour, every day with Will Shakespeare. I was in love, joyfully in love, and I believed he felt the same. At first we attempted to keep our love affair a secret, but that proved impossible. When I passed my twenty-sixth birthday on the first of August—Will gave me a little deerskin purse in honor of the day—we decided that we would no longer be bound by secrecy. Will asked to call upon me openly. I assented, but first I would have to tell Joan.

My stepmother was shocked, and not pleasantly so. "Have you lost your senses, Agnes?" she demanded. "You threw away a fine opportunity to marry a man who, though not without his faults, could have provided well for you. And now you waste your time on an idler lacking in both ambition and talent for hard work."

Stung, I railed at her. "Will Shakespeare lacks nothing!" I cried. "He's blessed with both a nimble mind and a strong back! Did you not see him laboring in the fields with the other men, or observe the care with which he selected kids for their fine skins? Did you not listen to him sing songs of his own composition, or hear him tell of writing and acting with the company of players? Have you not seen his well-made gloves? I believe Will Shakespeare can do whatever he chooses, and do it better than anyone."

Joan set aside the ale jugs she was cleansing. "Agnes,"

she said grimly, "heed my words: Will Shakespeare may be all that you say he is and more, but he is only eighteen years old and has many wild oats to sow before he takes a wife. You are six-and-twenty, rather late in the game for finding a husband—as I've been telling you for some time! Do not deceive yourself: Will Shakespeare will not marry you. As you've said yourself, he's a player, and players are little better than vagabonds. You are nothing to him but an interlude, an entertainment between acts. Nothing, nothing, nothing!"

Joan turned back to washing out the ale jugs, and I rushed out of the buttery and ran to the barn, where I tried to console myself. *She's wrong, she's wrong,* I whispered over and over. *Will loves me. That's all that matters.*

But another quiet voice inside my head intruded: *What if she's right?*

❦

The days passed in a golden haze, the nights in silvery splendor. Every Saturday evening and Sunday afternoon Will came to call. Ignoring Joan's sour looks and Joan Little's snickers, we went off together. Many times, both day and night, we returned to the thicket of young birches that grew close by Shottery Brook. The thicket was well hidden from the beaten path, and if someone happened along that path, we waited silently until the trespasser had passed by. It was our secret place, our private domain.

Sometimes Will brought his cittern and played for me. "Here's a new song," he said. "I was thinking of you when I wrote it."

> *Under the greenwood tree*
> *Who loves to lie with me,*
> *And turn her merry note*
> *Unto the sweet bird's throat,*
> *Come hither, come hither, come hither.*

The notes trailed off. "It's not finished yet. I plan several more stanzas. Do you like it?"

"I do."

"Then come hither and kiss me, Anne."

I did.

Ofttimes we spoke of our dreams and private desires. Mine were so common as to need no expression: a home, a loving husband, children. Will's were, to my way of thinking, far more fanciful.

"London!" he said. "Can you imagine it, Anne? That's where I want to be! You'd go with me, wouldn't you?"

Swept along by his enthusiasm, I agreed that I would—not from any real desire of my own to visit that vast, tumultuous, and surely dangerous city, but because, when Will spoke of London, I felt included in his plans for the future.

"They have playhouses in London, not at all like our crude innyards, and companies of players to perform in them. I dream of going there, and acting with a company, and mayhap writing lines for the players," he said, growing more excited with the telling of it. "You'd like that, too, would you not? Seeing the River Thames with its great ships arriving from all parts of the world, and London Bridge crossing over it, and St. Paul's Cathedral, and Westminster Abbey, and the Tower of London, and the queen's palaces—you'd want to see it all, would you not?"

"Aye," I said to please him. "I would like that."

We sometimes remained in that thicket for hours, unaware of the passage of time as we whispered words of love and exchanged caresses until the fading light reminded us that the day was nearly ended. When it rained, we found refuge in a nearby barn, though the risk of discovery made us uneasy. On Thursdays, after the closing bell of the market, I sometimes took the long way round to the glover's workshop behind the Shakespeares' barn, gambling that we would not be found.

Soon the glorious summer would come to an end. The sun had begun to set earlier, and the air to become cooler. But my love for Will continued to grow, and Will's kisses and caresses convinced me that his love for me grew as well, though he had not spoken of it in so many words—not the way he spoke of London and the players he wanted to be part of.

Then one afternoon in late August, my love having weakened my resolve, I yielded to our shared passion. My virgin-knot was broken.

I wept. Will tried to comfort me, but I could not be soothed. "It will not happen again," he promised, but what had been done could not be undone, what was lost could never be restored. Sick with shame, I sent him away.

There followed a week of remorse and despair. My stepmother's words haunted me: *Will Shakespeare will not marry you. You are nothing to him but an entertainment between the acts.* Sleepless, unhappy, I dragged myself through my chores with eyes red and swollen, certain everyone in our household had some notion of what had happened. Joan Little went about whistling a merry tune, and I thought she did it just to provoke me.

I worried that the bawdy court would learn of my transgression, for despite my threats, Joan Little had grown bolder. She must have guessed that the threats were empty, my power to punish her nonexistent. All she had to do was go to the Bishop's Council and report what she believed to be true about me. That it was *likely* true was all the proof they required.

The next Sunday Will returned, bringing a nosegay of flowers picked along the way. I refused the flowers and again told him to leave.

"Hear me out, dearest Anne," he begged. "I've written a poem for you—a sonnet."

I tried, without success, to harden my heart, but in the end I agreed to listen.

> *Those lips that love's own hand did make*
> *Breathed forth the sound that said "I hate"*
> *To me that languished for her sake;*
> *But when she saw my woeful state,*
> *Straight in her heart did mercy come,*
> *Chiding that tongue that ever sweet*
> *Was used in giving gentle doom,*
> *And taught it thus anew to greet:*
> *"I hate" she altered with an end,*
> *That followed it as gentle day*
> *Doth follow night, who like a fiend*
> *From heaven to hell is flown away.*
> *"I hate" from hate away she threw,*
> *And saved my life, saying "not you."*

Like a schoolboy Will glanced at me anxiously, waiting for my response. I was quick to give it.

"Nay, nay, I could never hate you, darling Will," I said. "You must know that I love you."

I kissed him, and he kissed me, and though I knew it was wrong and I would surely come to regret it, I yielded to our passion again, and more than once.

CHAPTER SIXTEEN
•*Regret*•

UMMER FADED. The gentle weather that seemed to bless our love now turned wet, cold, and punishing. No longer could we while away a pleasant hour or two in each other's arms under a blue and cloudless sky. We still sometimes took refuge in the neighbor's barn or the loft above the glover's workshop, but no place was safe from discovery. We were forced to be chaste, since the threat of the bawdy court put us at great peril.

I hoped this might work to my advantage: Mayhap Will's unsatisfied desire for me would prompt him to think of marriage. Will continued to call upon me on Saturday evenings and Sunday afternoons, reading me lines of poetry and singing new verses of songs. After the market closed, we walked together on the banks of the Avon if the weather was fair. But still he did not speak the words I yearned to hear: *Marry me, Anne.*

His apparent reluctance ignited in my heart a cold flame I had struggled to smother: jealousy. *Is he tiring of me? Has he met someone younger, someone more pleasing?* Thoughts of the girls who eagerly sought his attention at Thursday market and Sunday worship began to torment me. My suspicions settled upon Mariah Wotton, the younger sister of the recipient of Alexander Aspinall's excellent cheverel gloves. Mariah possessed a dark and sultry beauty. I'd heard that she played exquisitely upon the clavichord and sang sweetly as well. And she was just seventeen years old.

I could not sleep or eat. My stomach churned. The least thing caused me to burst into tears. Will seemed oblivious to my distress, and naturally I struggled to hide my misery from my family.

The weeks passed. We were well into autumn. What began as a faint unease turned to apprehension as several more weeks went by, and I felt ill nearly every day. By mid-October apprehension had grown to fear, and by All Hallows' Eve fear had become a hard knot of dread. Another anguished week went by. I counted and re-counted on my fingers. By my figuring, I was more than two months gone.

I tried to think how to tell Will that I was carrying a child. I could not discuss the matter with my step-mother, and I surely did not wish Joan Little to know of my predicament. I could confide in Catty, but though Catty was loving and loyal to me, hers was not a temperament suited to dealing with trouble. She would weep and hold my hand and weep some more; I would surely find myself consoling her, and my problem would be no nearer a solution.

On a damp November day I followed the muddy path to the thicket near the brook where Will and I had passed so many blissful summer hours. Now the black trees stood stark and bare, the earth littered with a mat of wet, brown leaves. I sat down on a lichen-crusted rock, pulled my shawl tighter, and tried to think through my unhappy circumstances.

Had I been betrothed to Will, the matter would not have been quite so serious. The church condemned such situations, though they were not unusual. I knew of several betrothed couples who'd been wed with the bride in a loose-waisted gown. But this was no help to me. Will and I were not betrothed, nor had there been a mention of marriage. When word of my condition got out, as surely it must, the bawdy court might well decide to chastise us both. Our families would suffer humiliation and shame. I would be disgraced. It was different for

Will—an unwed pregnancy was the woman's dishonor, not the man's. I sat shivering on the rock and pondered my gloomy future.

What if Will refuses to marry me, claiming he's too young?

What if he agrees to marry me out of duty, even though he doesn't want the responsibility of a wife and child?

What if he doesn't truly love me after all?

What if he loves Mariah Wotton?

My stomach heaved and my head throbbed. For a time I huddled in the barren thicket and wept. Then, chilled to the bone, I made my way back to the cottage, no closer to knowing what to do.

Finally, I decided to visit Emma. She would at least hear me out with a sympathetic ear, and mayhap she could advise me.

❦

That night it rained again, and though the rain had stopped before morning, threatening black clouds muffled the sky. Nevertheless, I set out early, telling Catty that I was going to the Whatleys in Temple Grafton and would return before nightfall.

In fair weather the hamlet was not much more than an hour's walk, but the rains had turned the path muddy and slick, and my progress was slow. I arrived at Emma's croft damp and weary. Emma greeted me with kisses and bade me rest by the fire while she heated some spiced ale for us both. Cicely, a cheerful little girl, toddled after her mother, regarding me with clear blue eyes like Emma's.

"I'm so glad you've come!" Emma said. "I had no notion to expect a visit from you." She handed me a steaming mug and an oatcake. "Oh, I miss you so! I do feel so alone here sometimes. Except for Cicely." She pulled the child onto her lap and nuzzled her thick curls. I watched enviously as mother and child nestled contentedly together.

I asked about Robin, and we whispered a bit about her mother-in-law who, I knew, must be lurking on the other side of the wall and might very well decide to draw a stool close to the connecting door to listen to our conversation.

When I laid aside the oatcake uneaten, Emma leaned forward and regarded me carefully. "Are you well, Agnes?" she asked. "You look a bit pale."

"An uneasy stomach," I said, and then, unable to hold back any longer, I burst into wrenching sobs.

Emma set Cicely on the floor and rushed to my side. "Oh, my dear Agnes, what is it?" she asked.

"I believe that I'm with child," I began. There were many necessary details to be filled in. When I had last seen Emma at May Day, we had discussed my planned marriage to Hob Ingram. Now she mistakenly believed that Hob was the cause of my trouble.

"Nay, not Hob Ingram," I said. "Will Shakespeare."

"Will Shakespeare!" Emma exclaimed. "You jest! Nay, I can see that you don't. To be truthful, I'm not surprised. I think you've been in love with him these two or three years, and he with you for twice as long! But how did this come about? When do you intend to wed? The sooner, the better, I'd say. I shall be in your wedding party, after all!"

I poured out the story. The more excited Emma became at the prospect of a wedding, the harder I wept. "So," she said, "have the banns been cried?" I shook my head. "Nay? But think, Agnes! We're well into November, the season of Advent begins in less than three weeks, and then no banns may be cried until after Twelfth Night. You won't be permitted to wed for two more months! What can Will be thinking, to postpone this!"

"Will doesn't know," I confessed at last.

"You haven't told him that you're expecting his child? Why on earth *not*?" she demanded.

"Because he's never spoken of marriage. He's only eighteen, have you forgotten? Legally, he's still an infant, with no more right to marry than your Cicely does. He must have his parents' permission. And what if he doesn't wish to marry me? What if he loves someone else?" I didn't mention my suspicions of Mariah Wotton. "It would surely mean the bawdy court, would it not? Oh, I can't bear the humiliation, Emma!" I burst into fresh tears.

"Agnes, you must tell him, and soon. Will loves you, of that I'm sure. He'll do the right thing by you." She hesitated. "But in the event he does show some reluctance, then you must tell my father of your plight. He is your godfather, remember, pledged to look out for you after your father's death." Emma took my hand and gazed at me earnestly. "'Tis what Richard Hathaway would want you to do."

❧

After a dinner of savory hotchpotch made with cabbage and barley that Emma swore was all she could keep down during her pregnancy, Emma and I talked, I helped her with her chores, and slowly I began to feel better. But I paid little attention to the hard rain that had begun to beat against the window, until I realized that I must leave quickly in order to reach Hewlands before fog and rain and gathering darkness made the way impossible to see. Emma begged me to stay the night with her; Robin and his father had gone to Worcester to thatch a large cottage and were not expected to return until the next day or the day after, depending upon the weather. But it was Saturday—Will usually came to call on Saturday nights—and I was eager to be at home when he arrived. I promised Emma that I would tell Will of my condition, and I made up my mind to do it that very night. There was no more time to waste.

Rashly, then, and against Emma's advice and her pleas that I must not leave in such weather, I kissed her and little Cicely and set out into the worsening storm.

I had intended to return by the Alcester Road, but that was the long way round. Taking the field path instead would save considerable time, and I struck out in the direction of Shottery. But the plowed field was waterlogged and crisscrossed with rivulets. Runnels that usually carried only small trickles of water were now ankle-deep, some even deeper.

Rain mixed with sleet, driven by a fierce wind, lashed me. Swirling fog erased familiar landmarks. Before long, I was hopelessly lost and shivering with cold. Soon darkness would fall, making matters worse. Frightened, I began to weep.

After a considerable time—what seemed like hours but was probably less—I stumbled onto a road. But which road was it? The Alcester Road? I was so confused that I could not think which way to turn: to the left or to the right? Then miraculously the fog thinned, and I recognized that I was near Drayton. It occurred to me that I could stop at the malthouse to rest before I continued on. Joan's brother Martin would surely take me in. The worst that could happen would be finding Hob Ingram there, too. The scene was sure to be unpleasant, but at least I'd be safe.

I had nearly decided to risk knocking on Martin's door, when I saw a solitary horse and rider approaching in the distance. I stood still, too weary to go another step, and watched them draw nearer. I thought I recognized the peculiar gait of my father's old horse, Copper, and I prayed it was Tolly who'd come looking for me. My legs shaking and about to give way under me, I raised my hand and waved to attract the rider's attention. The horse picked up its pace, stumbling and sliding toward me through the mud.

It was indeed my father's horse, but the rider wasn't Tolly. It was Will Shakespeare.

I must be dreaming this, I thought, until the next moment when Will leaped from the horse and began kissing me several times over as he enveloped me in his thick woolen cloak.

"Thank God I've found you, Anne! I came to Hewlands to see you, and Catty told me you'd gone to Emma's. Everyone else was sure you'd stay there for the night, but Catty insisted you'd come back. Tolly was ready to ride out looking for you, but I told him to go on home to Isabella and let me come instead. He loaned me your father's horse."

Will lifted me onto Copper's back, sprang up behind me, and turned Copper toward home. Exhausted, I leaned against Will's chest and drowsed. We said little until at last I recognized the dark silhouette of the cottage and barn. I stayed with Will as he stalled the horse and filled its leather bucket with oats. My teeth were chattering, and I was shivering, but I held back when Will put his arm round me and began to hurry me toward the cottage.

"Will," I said, "stay one moment longer. I've something to say."

"Can it not wait until you've warmed yourself by the fire and had something hot to drink? You'll surely take a chill."

"Nay, it cannot wait." I drew one or two breaths to steady my voice before trying to speak. This was not a time for weakness or for weeping. When I felt calm, I said, "I am expecting a child, Will. Our child."

The light in the barn had grown so dim that I could not make out Will's features. I was aware of the loud beating of my heart as I waited for his reply. For a long moment he said nothing. When he spoke, it was to ask a question: "Are you certain?"

"Aye, I'm certain. I'm past two months along."

Another long silence. I had nearly given up the hope that he would speak the words I longed to hear: *Marry me, Anne.* My heart was ready to break. *He loves Mariah Wotton,* I thought. *Not me.*

"I won't tell you an untruth—I hadn't counted upon this," he said at last. "But—," he began, stopped, and began again. "Dearest Anne, will you consent to be my wife?"

"Aye," I whispered. "I will."

"Then kiss me, Anne."

I kissed him, a sweet kiss, a tender kiss, but a kiss with more relief than passion.

❧

Will had asked me to marry him and I had accepted, but when the storm subsided and he returned to Stratford that night, we still had made no plans. I knew that he would need his father's permission to marry. What if John Shakespeare refused that permission? Suppose he and Mary didn't want Will to marry me, hoping that in five years or ten their eldest son would contract a marriage with a girl from a family of rank and wealth.

The next day, Sunday, I felt unwell and did not walk to Holy Trinity with the others. Nor did Will call upon me that afternoon, as he usually did.

"Where's your sweetheart? Afraid of a little rain?" asked Joan Little. I prayed that she hadn't guessed the cause of it. By the time the rush candle had burned out, I had given up the notion that Will might yet come.

I didn't speak of our agreement to anyone, nor did I tell anyone of my condition. The days dragged by with no word from Will, and I began to worry all over again. The nights were even longer, for I slept little, tossing restlessly on my pallet and keeping Catty awake, too. I saw my stepmother's suspicious eye upon me as we went about our daily chores and in the evenings when we'd lit a rush candle and tended to our spinning, our knitting and mending.

The spell of bad weather was interrupted on Thursday by a period of warm, sunny days that my father used to call St. Martin's summer, a welcome break before winter's hard jaws closed. Still there was no word from Will. *Has he changed his mind?* I fretted. *What am I to do?*

On the third of these mild days—Saturday, marking a week since I had spoken to Will—Fulke Sandells and John Richardson appeared at the door of the cottage, asking for me. Meg summoned me from the buttery, where Joan and my sisters and I were making cheese. They watched curiously as I wiped my hands on my apron and went to meet the callers. I stepped outside and closed the door, aware that my stepmother and sisters had paused to listen.

"Good morrow, Goodman Sandells and Goodman Richardson," I said, trying not to show my nervousness.

"Well met, Agnes," the two men replied as one.

Time had worn deep furrows in Fulke's kindly face. John was stooped, his beard streaked white. We spoke a little of the beauty of the day, the remarkable fineness of the weather. I didn't immediately invite them into the hall but decided to wait until they'd had their say.

"We've had a conversation with John Shakespeare," the weaver began. "And with William. They told us that Will has proposed marriage to you, and that you have accepted his proposal. Is't true, Agnes?"

"Aye, 'tis." I clasped my hands tightly to still them.

John Richardson glanced at Fulke Sandells, who took up the narrative. "William also admitted, with some prodding, that you are with child and that he wants to get on with the wedding as soon as practical. But, as you know, the church requires the banns to be cried for three weeks running, to assure that no prior marriage contract exists for either party, or any other reason why the marriage should not go forward. But 'tis only two weeks until the start of Advent, during which no banns may be cried or wedding vows exchanged."

I nodded that I understood.

"As I'm sure you know, William is not of age to marry without his parents' consent. They were quite willing to give consent and agreed that the wedding must take place without delay."

The tightness in my chest loosened.

The weaver sighed. "But to do that, a surety bond of forty pounds must be posted as a guarantee to the diocese of Worcester that there is no—what was the word, Fulke?"

"Impediment," Fulke supplied. "No *impediment* to the marriage. 'Tis quite a lot of money, Agnes. More than our earnings for the year. John Shakespeare could find no one to loan him such a large amount. When he came to us, we agreed to loan the money, out of respect for your late father."

"Aye," John Richardson acknowledged, "that we did. And now that it's settled, we're prepared to accompany you and young Shakespeare to Worcester to post the bond and request a special license to marry without the crying of the banns. Whenever you're ready," he said. Then he added, "But there's not much time left."

I thanked them over and over for their kindness. "I will never forget you for this," I said. "But now I must talk to Will." I watched them leave. Nearly overcome with a heady mixture of shame, relief, and joy, I tried to collect myself before I returned to the buttery.

"What did those two want of you?" Joan asked.

I took a deep breath. "They came to tell me that I'm to marry Will Shakespeare before the month is out," I said and continued to squeeze the whey from the curds, though my heart was full to bursting and I felt anything but calm.

"Marry Will Shakespeare!" my stepmother exclaimed, dropping the cheese sieve with a clatter. "You've surely gone mad!"

Catty gaped, openmouthed. Joan Little stared. I began to laugh. "Nay, Stepmother, not mad—quite sane, and quite happy. And you shall get your wish at last."

Later I would tell them of my circumstances. But not now. I wanted to savor this moment—my family's surprise and amazement, my own joy and relief. Practical matters could wait for another time.

CHAPTER SEVENTEEN
·*Marriage*·

N THE day after the visit from my father's friends and eight long days after his promise to marry me, Will appeared again at Hewlands. I ran out to greet him.

"Come walk with me, Anne," he said, reaching for my hand.

The late November day was still unseasonably warm. We walked straight to the thicket where we had spent so many blissful summer hours, the same thicket where I'd sat upon a rock and wept and prayed. Now Will sat upon that rock and pulled me onto his lap.

"Remember how pleasantly the birds sang when we last came here?" he asked.

"Aye, I do."

"How sweet the summer was for us. And how sweet the winter will be, once we're wed." He gazed at the bare branches above us and the carpet of dead leaves beneath our feet. Then he turned his dark eyes to me. "Kiss me, Anne."

Once we're wed. It was what I wanted to hear. I kissed him gladly and rested my head upon his shoulder. There were still immediate plans to be made, but Will seemed a good deal more interested in lovemaking than he was in arranging a wedding. Nevertheless, at my urging, by the time the sun had dipped low on the horizon and a chill wind had begun to gnaw at the edges of our thicket, we had agreed that on the coming Wednesday we would ride to Worcester with my father's friends to obtain the special license. Three days later, the first of December, we would marry at St. Andrew's in Temple Grafton, avoiding the curious stares we'd surely receive if we married at Holy Trinity in Stratford. If Will knew of Vicar John Frith's reputation as a believer in the old faith, he gave no sign, and I was unwilling to mention it.

Now that my future was assured, I again felt easy with him. "Where shall we live, my love?" I asked my soon-to-be husband.

For some time I had dreamed of a home of my own, and as the years passed I came to see it clearly: a simple croft with a fire blazing on the hearth, a snug loft for sleeping with my husband by my side and a babe in the cradle, a garth next to the cottage with a garden plot for herbs and vegetables and a few fowl, a byre for a cow or two, a fold for several sheep and goats, a bee-stall near a lavender field, mayhap even a rose-covered bower. It would be a small place but blessedly uncrowded with a dour stepmother and her sneering daughter and all the other brothers and sisters, shepherds and servants who made their home at Hewlands. I smiled now, as I imagined our home.

"With my parents," Will replied.

"Your parents?" I drew back in surprise. "We are to live with your parents?"

I could scarcely hide my disappointment as my dream shattered. I was fond of Mary Shakespeare and thought well of John, but their household also included three younger brothers and a sister—eight of us, nine after the birth of my infant—in addition to a number of servants and apprentices. I would be leaving one crowded, noisy, bustling household for another, not my own.

"They will make you most welcome, I promise you," Will said. "And we have no means to do otherwise."

I attempted to smile. "Aye, I know."

Will must have sensed my disenchantment. "Be patient, Anne, I beg you. Someday we'll have a place to call our own."

"Aye," I said, thinking, *He's only eighteen. Still only a boy. Still his parents' son.* I sighed and bit my trembling lip.

"Kiss me, Anne," he said, turning my face toward his, tipping up my chin.

And I did.

❦

The warm, sunny days ended abruptly with a heavy frost, a harbinger of the coming winter. Well before sunrise on the twenty-eighth of November, I stood waiting for Will. The household was grimly silent. My stepmother refused to speak to me. Her silence was a welcome relief after the scolding I had endured since I'd finally confessed to her that I was expecting a child.

"What a disgrace you are!" she'd cried. "Not that I'm surprised. You always were a bad one. I warned your father about you since the first day I set foot in this house, but he would hear no complaint about his dear little Agnes! Well, wouldn't he change his tune now! I'm just glad—*glad*—that blameless man didn't live to see the dishonor you've brought on his family and his good name."

I'd said nothing while she raved, choosing instead to close my ears and let her spew her fury. Soon I would be gone from Hewlands, and her wrath would no longer matter.

Will arrived at last, accompanied by a stern-faced John Richardson and a somber Fulke Sandells. All were on horseback, and they'd brought a horse for me; Copper was too old to make the forty-mile journey to Worcester and back. I hurried out to meet them, and we were on our way, the horses' hooves ringing on the frozen ground.

The two older men were in no mood for pleasantries. One rode beside Will, the other beside me—afraid, I suppose, that Will was a reluctant bridegroom who might bolt if not under escort. For them this was an obligation. They plainly saw nothing here to celebrate. Will himself seemed distracted and far away, though occasionally he turned to smile at me. I tried to keep my spirits up, picturing our wedding.

We arrived in Worcester before noon and found the way to the cathedral on the Severn River. We had a long wait until the harried clerk in the diocesan court office entered our names in his registry book, after first mistaking me for a girl named Whatley from Temple Grafton. The clerk blotted his book and delivered the proper license—not to Will, who was underage, but to Fulke, once the bond had been posted. It was already too late to start for home. We ate a silent supper of greasy mutton and put up for the night at a wayside inn.

Except for the two nights I'd slept in our wagon during the queen's visit to Kenilworth—so long ago!—this was the first time I had not spent the night on my pallet in our cottage. Will and the two men shared a room with an itinerant tinker. I shared a bed with a woman traveling with her two daughters to visit a third. The bed was lumpy, the blanket shrunken, and the woman a loud snorer. I lay sleepless as the watchman called the hours in the street below our window, thinking of what the future might hold. I thought of the babe growing in my belly and wondered what it would be like. Boy or girl? And what would we name it? So far we had not spoken at all of the child.

We left Worcester the next morning. The road to Stratford led through Alcester and a mile or two farther on passed the turning to Temple Grafton. Here our two escorts, eager to get home, agreed to continue on without us, while Will and I took the road to Temple Grafton to speak to the vicar of St. Andrew's. Alone now, we were suddenly shy with each other.

We knocked and waited as the old priest made his way slowly to the door of the vicarage. Vicar John Frith looked us up and down with rheumy eyes. Finally he stepped back and ushered us inside. I noticed a peculiar smell; then I saw that the vicar was not alone. Birds of prey of various kinds—kestrels, goshawks, a peregrine falcon—roosted in corners of the small, spare chamber. There were three stools; we took two, and Vicar John seated himself upon the third. A small barn owl swooped down out of the shadows to perch on the vicar's shoulder and regarded us with lively interest.

Will explained the reason for our visit. By the light of a rush candle Vicar John squinted at the license, which Fulke had entrusted to me. "Ten o'clock in the forenoon on Saturday, the first day of December," he rasped. He dismissed us amid a flapping of wings.

Outside the vicarage Will and I looked at each other and broke into relieved laughter. I wondered aloud if the barn owl would be in attendance on Saturday. "If it is, it will surely bring us luck," Will said, and clasped me tightly.

We untied our horses from the rail. "Now," I said, my mood much lightened, "I must stop and have a word with Emma. I'll need her help if we're to have a wedding in two days' time."

We appeared at Emma's door, still laughing, and explained the reason for our visit. With a happy cry, Emma embraced us both. She summoned Robin from the barn, offered us bread, meat, and ale, and said, "Now, prithee, begin at the beginning. The day after tomorrow, aye?"

By the time we left to make our way home in the early darkness, Emma had everything planned: I would return the next day with ribbons bought from the mercer in Stratford. We would gather greens and Emma would make me a bridal wreath. I would borrow her best bodice and petticoats, as there was no time to make my own. At ten o'clock the following morning our families would gather at the church for the ceremony. Afterward, all would go to the Blue Boar Inn by the Alcester Road for a dinner, which Will and I would arrange. Emma's cheeks were pink with pleasure, as though she herself were again a bride.

"Now go," she commanded us, "and invite whomever you wish to the wedding. And Will," she added, shaking her finger, "remember to buy the rings!"

Though they had seen us off the day before, my sisters could still not fully believe that I was about to be married—and to Will Shakespeare. Joan no longer raved, but she did continue to grumble. "'Tis a sorry mess you've made of things. He's sure to leave you for the first pretty face to catch his fancy."

I remembered what my stepmother had once said to me of Will: *You are nothing to him but an entertainment between acts.* Those harsh words came back to me now.

Catty was the one to banish the clouds that Joan had conjured. She seized my hands and danced me in a circle. "I'm angry at Will Shakespeare!" she cried. "He's taking you away from me!" She let go my hands. "Oh,

Agnes, I shall miss you so much. But I know that you will be happy."

I thanked her for her good wishes, knowing that she must feel as I had felt when Emma married Robin and moved to Temple Grafton. "But I shall not go far, dear Catty, I promise you. Now come with me to town. I've shopping to do, and I need your help."

❧

And so on the bright, cold morning of the first of December in 1582, William Shakespeare led me to St. Andrew's Church where Vicar John Frith waited. I wore the bridal wreath Emma had fashioned for me and the kidskin gloves Will had once given me, and I felt as a bride should feel—happy, excited, and in love. In the presence of our families—including Joan and Joan Little, with matching sour expressions—and a few close friends and well-wishers, we exchanged our vows. Will placed a gold ring upon my finger and honored me with a matrimonial kiss.

I was now a married woman, wife of William Shakespeare.

As we left the church I whispered to Will, "No owl."

"Our luck will still be good," Will assured me. "How could it be otherwise?"

All of the Shakespeares had turned out for the ceremony and the dinner that followed. Samuel and Alys Fletcher had come. Fulke Sandells was there, though Martha was feeling weak and sent her regrets. John Richardson and his wife came; so did Stephen and his bride, the girl from Tiddington—perhaps thirty people in all. At the Blue Boar we ate meat pies and frumenty and drank spiced cider. Tolly proposed a toast, as did John Shakespeare. Will played the cittern while Catty and Emma and Will's sister Joan sang one of his songs.

> *This carol they began that hour,*
> *With a hey, and a ho, and a hey-nonny-no,*
> *How that a life was but a flower,*
> *When birds do sing, hey ding-a-ding, ding;*
> *Sweet lovers love the spring…*

To surprise us, Tolly and Isabella had decorated a wagon with greens and tied ribbons to the horns of the oxen who pulled it. In this conveyance my husband—*my husband!*—and I left the Blue Boar among the cheers of well-wishers and drove to Henley Street in Stratford-upon-Avon to begin our life together.

❧

John and Mary Shakespeare had returned home earlier and were there to greet us. My father-in-law gave us his blessing, and my mother-in-law made me feel warmly welcome in the household. "My dear Anne—shall I call you Anne, as Will does?—what delight it gives me to have you as part of our family." If she thought ill of me that I had gotten with child before I was wed, she gave no sign of it, and I loved her for that.

It was a lively home with Gilbert, two years younger than Will; Joan, thirteen; Dick, eight; and two-year-old Edmund. Will spent his days in his father's workshop making not only gloves but purses, bags, belts, and sword-hangers. When he had a few spare moments, he crept up to the loft and scribbled poems. During the long winter evenings I sat by the fire and sewed the tiny garments that I would soon need for my infant, and Will plucked the strings of lute or cittern and tried out new verses to songs he was composing. Those were peaceful, happy times.

In April Will observed his nineteenth birthday; a month later I gave birth to our daughter. On Trinity Sunday, May twenty-eighth, she was carried to Holy Trinity and baptized Susannah, with Catty as her proud godmother and Gilbert as godfather. Afterward John and Mary saw to it that the christening of their first grandchild was properly celebrated, and the guest list was long and included everyone in my family. Susannah lay wide-eyed in the Shakespeare family cradle where I remembered seeing her father as an infant, and then his brothers and sisters in turn. The spread was ample, if not as sumptuous as on earlier occasions, for John's circumstances were tight. I was certain my stepmother must have noted this fact with satisfaction and commented upon it after she left.

❧

Before my marriage I'd seized every opportunity to escape the farm for the busy hum of town life. But once I'd come to live in the midst of all the noise and bustle of Stratford-upon-Avon, I often yearned for the quiet of the countryside, unbroken by clamoring bells at the Guild Hall, the cries of the night watchman on his rounds, the shouts of quarrelsome drunks ousted from nearby inns.

Though I sometimes missed Hewlands, I didn't miss my life there with Joan and Joan Little one whit. I did sometimes miss Tom and the others, but Catty now spent so much time visiting me and her infant niece that it was as though she, too, had become a member of the family.

"Do you recall," I once asked Mary Shakespeare, "after our mother died, you offered to have Catty come and live with you?"

"I do, indeed," Mary replied. "I would have liked nothing more. But now I have you and Susannah with me, and Catty as often as she pleases. I am truly blessed."

I, too, felt blessed. I was satisfied in my new role as wife and mother, and even more content when I found myself again pregnant before Susannah was a year old. Our twins, named Judith and Hamnet in honor of our friends who stood as their godparents, were christened on Candlemas, 1585. I was eight-and-twenty. Will was only twenty and already the father of three.

❧

I had grown to love my husband ever more deeply, and I believed that he loved me as well. He seemed sincerely devoted to our children. But I was keenly aware of Will's mounting restlessness.

In the year after the twins were born, several companies of players passed through Stratford. Will seldom missed a performance, spent time conversing with the players, and occasionally got small parts to play. As long as the company was in town, Will was in high spirits; after they'd moved on, his mood plunged. When I arose during the night to nurse the two infants, I would find Will awake and pacing. It was plain that he was dissatisfied with his life.

I worried and wondered what I could do. Somehow we kept on. The year of the twins' second birthday, five companies played in Stratford-upon-Avon, among them Leicester's Men from Kenilworth and the Queen's Men, down from London. Will knew many of the actors by then and caroused a night or two away with them at a nearby inn before they went on to the next town. But not, apparently, before they had urged him to join up with them.

We talked in whispers as the three little ones slept on pallets near our bed. "The players say the best chances for employment with a company are in London," Will murmured close to my ear. "They tell me there's plenty of work for a man willing to take on odd jobs near the playhouses, and with luck one might get to act a bit, and even to write, if one has the talent for it. And I do, Anne! I know that I can make a success of it, given the chance. Nothing will ever come of it if I spend my life at the glover's bench."

"But it would take you away from us," I whispered, staring into the darkness. Apprehension lay like a cold stone upon my stomach. "And who knows for how long?"

"Aye, for months, 'tis true. But then I would come home again to you, dearest Anne, satisfied that I've had my hour upon the stage."

Satisfied? I knew well enough that Will would not be satisfied with a mere taste. He would want to consume the whole meal, the entire banquet! But I said nothing of that. Instead, my mind and body aching to snatch a little rest, I said, "Sleep now, dear Will, and we'll talk again later."

And we did talk again, many times. The discussion was always the same: the opportunities, the challenges, but never the risks that I saw. These discussions became more heated, sometimes ending angrily. Each time I realized that Will's will (how aptly he had been named!) was stronger than ever. I remembered a time when he was still a boy of thirteen, and I had walked with him along the field path from Shottery; he'd told me that he would one day be a poet. And years later, when we'd become lovers, he'd told me of his desire to go to London to write and to act. The dream had been there all along, he'd spoken of it frankly, and I hadn't taken it seriously!

Finally, because I believed it might be the only way to keep his love, I agreed that he must go to London. I understood that, if I did not agree, he might indeed stay in Stratford with me—not out of desire, but out of duty. That would turn our once-sweet love to sour dregs, and I couldn't bear the thought. I knew I would bind him to me more firmly by letting him go.

"Then go, Will," I said. "'Tis something you must do, and I will not stand in your way."

"You're certain?" he asked. "My parents will look after you and the children until I return. You'll want for nothing. You won't be lonely."

Not lonely? How could I not be lonely without my husband? "We'll be fine," I lied, smiling bravely. "Go, Will."

And so, one fine day as the summer of 1587 drew to an end, Will prepared to leave for London. He kissed his son and two daughters, who had no notion of what their father was determined to do. Then he kissed his parents, who had every notion of it and were sternly disapproving. He shouldered his leather knapsack packed with his cittern, a few articles of clothing, and a book or two—I was to send the rest when he found lodgings—and picked up a walking stick he'd carved of alderwood. He believed he could reach London in four days, five at most, by walking eight to ten hours a day and sleeping at wayside inns. He was ready, and obviously eager, to be off.

I accompanied Will to the far end of the Clopton Bridge. "Fare thee well, dearest wife," he said tenderly. "I'll write to you, and mayhap you will write to me as well. And I will come back to you as soon as I can, I swear it!"

"Fare thee well, dear husband," I said with a calmness I didn't feel, determined that I would not spoil his leaving with the sobs that were welling up in my breast.

"Kiss me, Anne," said Will, and I did.

I watched with a breaking heart as Will started down the road toward London. He turned once and waved, and then he was gone. He did not look back.

CHAPTER EIGHTEEN
•Coming Home•

ILL DID not return to Stratford-upon-Avon for nearly a twelvemonth. During that time I learned to do without a husband. On market days I often went to help Catty at my old stall, and when it closed she came to have dinner with the Shakespeares. I worked at the glover's shop, keeping the inventory in order, and sometimes wrote letters for John, though I seldom wrote to Will. What was there to say? *I miss you, the children need you, I want you here, this is no marriage at all.* His letters were rare as well, most of them addressed to the family as a whole with affectionate words for the children.

Then one day he wrote that he was coming home—"for a visit." he said, though he didn't say for how long.

As eagerly as I looked forward to his homecoming, I worried, too. I was no longer the comely young woman he had wooed. *Lips like cherries,* he'd once said; *skin pale as a lily tinted with a primrose blush, eyes the very shade of bluebells.* Every one of my two-and-thirty years was plainly written on my face. Will on the other hand was a young man in his prime. I still could not forget my stepmother's words: *You are nothing to him but an entertainment between acts.* And yet, just as in the old days, I could hardly wait to see him, to hear his voice, to touch him.

When at last Will did come home, his children scarcely recognized him—he'd grown a beard, his hair was cut long, his breeches and doublet were the garb of a city man. His parents and I rushed out to greet him when he rode up, but Susannah, now a tempestuous five-year-old, glowered at him from a corner, and the twins, aged three and a half, wailed. He swept us all into his embrace—I was weeping joyful tears—and slowly the children came round and allowed his kisses.

My husband was brimming with passion for his new life. "I've held horses for patrons of the playhouse," he told the family as we gathered round him that evening, hanging on his words. His children, gradually accustomed to this interesting stranger, shyly leaned upon his knee and gazed up at him. "I've carried slops, I've shoveled and scrubbed and performed all manner of cheerless work, but at long last I progressed to the prompter's box—and from there to the stage itself."

"Are you acting, then, Will?" his father asked.

"So far only small parts," Will acknowledged. "More importantly, I've been writing!" he told us. "I've completed two history plays and one comedy and started another, and I have ideas for several more. All I need is time." He smiled at me and squeezed my hand, and I did my best to smile back.

That night I welcomed Will to our bed, and he seemed glad enough to be there.

He talked eagerly of the excitement of London: the sights, the sounds, the smells—even the filth and decay seemed to stimulate him. I knew from the first day of his homecoming that he would not remain with us for long. *All I need is time,* he'd said. And, indeed, within a fortnight he was preparing to leave again, having told me little of where he lived, who his friends were, or—most important—when he might come home again. He did say, though, as we parted once again at the end of the Clopton Bridge, that the Queen's Men frequently traveled out from London. "I hope that one day soon I'll perform with them here in Stratford."

"Aye, Will, and we'll be here to applaud," I said with a counterfeit smile, not truly believing that he would but pretending to believe, pretending that all was well.

When it comes to playacting, I thought, *I'm sure I could do as well as any of the Queen's Men.*

Then he kissed me and the children who clung to my skirts in bewilderment as the father they'd just come to know left them again. Miserably we made our way back to the Shakespeare house, where Catty was waiting for us.

"I don't see how you can bear it," she said, once the children had been soothed with a sweetmeat and sent off to play. "It's plain you're as much in love with Will as you ever were, and yet he's left you alone here again." My sister was soon to be handfasted to an usher in the lower school. She'd found a schoolteacher to marry after all.

"I *can't* bear it," I confessed. "But I suffer the pain and do what I must."

At Yuletide Will wrote, promising to return for the twins' fourth birthday in February. But he failed to appear, showing up instead a few months later for Susannah's sixth. I ached for him, but once I came to accept that my husband's visits home would be few and far between, I became accustomed to his absence. He regularly sent sums of money, so that we were not in want so long as we continued to make our home with his parents. My children grew and thrived and were a source of joy to me and to Will's parents, especially Mary.

The years passed. Catty married, and I stood as godmother for the christening of her firstborn, a daughter named Agnes for our mother. My son Hamnet entered the King's New School where Catty's husband was an usher. He assured me the boy had inherited his father's brilliance. I saw Tolly and Isabella and their children at sheepshearings and other feasts. Tom had finished his apprenticeship and now worked with his uncle, Samuel Fletcher; sometimes he came by the glover's shop and passed the time of day with me. Only rarely did I cross paths with Joan or Joan Little, who married an idler with an overfondness for drink. Will fell into a pattern of coming home each summer for a fortnight; I no longer expected more. Once or twice he suggested that I bring the children to London for a visit. I never did. Mayhap I should have, but the prospect of traveling to that sprawling, brawling city was too frightening.

I recognized that my Will Shakespeare, the witty, lighthearted boy I had fallen in love with, had become William Shakespeare, the famous playwright, his works often performed for the pleasure of Queen Elizabeth herself and drawing huge crowds to the playhouses. Sometimes he wrote to me with news of the opening of a new play. I've saved all his letters—there are not many—in that same wooden coffer my father once made for me. I read them with some ease, but I seldom wrote back.

The most difficult letter I ever had to write was in the summer of 1596 when Hamnet fell gravely ill. We did everything we could to save him—bled him, applied leeches, fed him mixtures prescribed by the apothecary. I begged Will to come home before it was too late. For days and nights the boy hung between life and death, while Catty stayed by my side. Will arrived in time to bury our only son, just eleven years old, on the eleventh of August.

We stared at each other across the open grave. Finally, when the gravediggers came to finish their work, Catty led me away. Will stayed behind, alone with his thoughts. We spoke little while he was in Stratford that time, and for the first time I did not accompany him across the Clapton Bridge when he left again for London. My grief prevented me from reaching out to him. I blamed him for not being there when Hamnet became ill. It's possible that he blamed himself.

The loss of our son seemed to bring about a change in Will, as though in his anguish he'd come to appreciate home and family and mayhap even his marriage in a way he had not during the nine years since he'd first taken the road to London. Not long after Hamnet's death, Will decided to buy a permanent home in Stratford. By then he could well afford the finest house in town and bought New Place, a handsome brick edifice of ten rooms with furnishings as well as a barn and gardens and orchards that much pleased me, though 'tis a far cry from my youthful wish for a simple croft in the country with a cow and a few sheep! But Will had no sooner moved me and Susannah and Judith out of his parents' home in Henley Street where we'd lived all those years and into these beautiful rooms than he rushed back to London—to a mistress, I supposed, though I never asked. I thought it better not to know.

Even with his purchase of New Place, my husband has remained but an occasional visitor to his own home, coming down from London for a fortnight or so each summer to renew acquaintance with his family and to saunter through the familiar streets of Stratford-upon-Avon, visiting boyhood haunts, greeting old friends and new admirers, and then returning to London.

"Can you not come oftener?" I had pleaded when the children were young. "Or stay longer?"

"But sweetheart," he'd explained, too many times, "'tis a two-day hard ride by fastest horse, and I have my obligations to the theater. Know that you and the children are never far from my thoughts."

I doubted that.

And so the years went by, I long ago stopped pleading, and now it is 1611. Will has passed his forty-seventh birthday; I shall soon observe my fifty-fifth. We've been married twenty-nine years, twenty-four of which Will has spent away from me in London.

And now, it seems, Will Shakespeare has decided to come home to stay. *I have given up my lodgings and arranged shipment of my belongings,* he has written to me from the city, *including a handsome new bed that I commissioned to be made for us by a London joiner. They should arrive within the fortnight, and I not long after. Then, my dear, all will change.*

In fact, all has already changed. John and Mary Shakespeare are dead and buried, as is my stepmother. Our daughter Susannah married John Hall, a physician and a good man, leaving Judith and me alone in the splendid house on Chapel Street. We have our own company, our own lives. And Will is coming home!

Well, then, let him come. I shall welcome him as I always have—with love and hope—for what may be the final chapter in our story.

ILLIAM SHAKESPEARE, the most celebrated poet and playwright in the English language, returned to Stratford-upon-Avon in 1611, where he continued to write until his death five years later. He died on April 23, 1616, a date generally believed to be his fifty-second birthday, and was buried in the chancel of Holy Trinity Church. Anne Hathaway Shakespeare died on August 11, 1623, at the age of sixty-seven. Their younger daughter, Judith, married Thomas Quiney, just weeks before her father died. Will and Anne have no direct descendants.

More books have been written about Shakespeare than about any other writer in the world, yet very little is known about his life. And what little is "known" often turns out to be controversial or simply a myth; we are left with only a handful of documented dates. Around this flimsy skeleton biographers and interpreters have attempted to construct a life.

Although April 23, 1564, is generally celebrated as Shakespeare's birthday, that date is really just another guess—there are no records to prove it. We do know, though, that he was christened on April 26, the date inscribed in the parish record book. And we know that babies were usually christened three days after they were born—unless that day was deemed unlucky, or for some other reason the baptism was postponed.

There is no proof that little Will Shakespeare attended the King's New School, although it's likely that he did, nor is it known for how long he might have been enrolled. Queen Elizabeth did make a royal visit to Kenilworth Castle in 1573. Was Will there? Probably, but there's no documentation if he was. Did he actually go to teach in Lancashire in 1581 when he was not quite seventeen? Someone named Shakespeare did, but it might not have been our Will.

The records concerning Will's marriage to Anne Hathaway are similarly unreliable. Information about Anne herself is sketchy. We do know who posted the surety bond for the hurry-up license, and approximately when the wedding took place. However, the christening dates of their children are a matter of record.

Just when and under what circumstances Will left Stratford-upon-Avon for London is anybody's guess. Some say he joined a troupe of players; others suggest that he had been caught poaching; in any event, sometime in the late 1580s William Shakespeare showed up in London, and soon his plays began to appear on the stage. There is disagreement about the order in which the plays were written, when they were first performed, and even if Will actually wrote them all!

The day of Will Shakespeare's death is a matter of record, but his last will and testament has raised more questions than it has answered about his relationship to his wife. With no tender words or explanations, he left her only the "second-best bed." Scholars ever since have argued about whether this was because it was actually more comfortable than the best bed, or Susannah and her husband needed the "best bed"—or Will simply believed it was appropriate for a wife who, herself, he deemed only "second best."

Whatever the ordinary facts of Shakespeare's life may have been, they are forever eclipsed by his extraordinary brilliance in capturing the range of human experience in his poetry and plays.